THE CASE OF THE PILFERING POLTERGEIST

A PARANORMAL COZY MYSTERY

B I SKINNER

CONTENTS

1

"That's rude!" I shout, shaking my fist at a slovenly poltergeist who just threw a yellow teddy bear at a small boy cowering behind a display shelf.

The greasy, shaggy-haired spirit is wearing a food-stained t-shirt and jeans with holes. The holes aren't there on purpose either. His messy hair has clearly gone un-cut since, well, long before he died.

He pauses mid-air, shocked when he realizes I can see him. He drops the Barbie he was holding in his other hand and flies over to me.

"Heyyyy," he grunts. "You can see me!"

"I can. I insist you stop terrorizing these people," I admonish, hands planted firmly on my hips, glaring at him through my angry, lavender eyes. Yes, my eyes are lavender. No, no one knows where I got them. Everyone else in my family had normal-colored eyes.

I say *had* because my parents died when I was ten years old. There were no other relatives, so I spent the rest of my youth in the foster care system. As an adult, most people find my eye coloring unique and exciting. As a child, however, the other kids picked on me. They insisted I was a witch. If they only knew!

The poltergeist hovers inches from my face. I'm grateful that spirits don't give off an odor, not to the living anyway, because I'm confident this one would smell like things I'd rather not think about. It makes my nose wrinkle just imagining it.

"I've never met one of you in person! You're one of them whatchamacallits." He silently snaps his luminescent fingers.

"I'm a spirit communicator," I confirm.

"Yeah, that's it. Spirit communicator. So, what brings you to these parts?"

Now that he's stopped throwing things, an elderly couple hiding behind a solid oak bookshelf ventures out. Upon seeing that, however, he grabs a paperback on the history of dolls and throws it in their direction, forcing them to retake their cover.

"*Please* stop doing that!" I insist.

"But it's fun!" he retorts.

"For you, maybe, but not for the innocent people you're antagonizing."

"Well, duh!" he laughs.

I give my friend Wendy the high sign that she should help the doll museum patrons hiding under the counter escape while I distract the poltergeist. So far, he's only throwing objects that can't injure them, but they're scared, and I understand why. They can't see the poltergeist like I can, much less talk to him. They just know that dolls, and other display items are flying through the air, forcing them to duck and cover.

Poltergeists are such a hassle. They're well known for their pranks and antagonistic behavior. But sometimes, they're dangerous and even deadly. Traditional ghosts exist because they never went into the light after they died and are confined to a particular place.

But poltergeists are created from negative energy. While they often attach themselves to a specific person or place that bears an abundance of negative energy, the more powerful poltergeists move about freely. Also, unlike traditional spirits, poltergeists enjoy tormenting their victims. They get a charge out of scaring people.

Mr. Beasley, the doll museum owner, has hired me to work with them to negotiate a truce. While the Glenwood Doll Museum has a well-documented history of hauntings, Mr. Beasley claims they've been behaving worse than ever lately. They've always caused trouble here but haven't been overly destructive or violent.

He explained how things are misplaced or hidden, but he just goes along with it because that's how poltergeists are. Recently, however, their behavior is dark and moody. He wants to know why. Last week, he found several nude dolls placed in obnoxious poses that weren't appropriate for public viewing.

He had to delay opening the museum that morning to locate their clothing, which he finally found hidden in the microwave, re-dress the dolls, then return them to their proper places. Today's disturbance is particularly troublesome because it's the first time they're willing to injure people and damage property.

I'm here to assess the situation and determine a plan for the museum. My friends Wendy and Juliet insisted on coming with me because they're witches. I'm hopeful they'll have a spell to subdue a vengeful spirit. They're two of the first people I met when I moved to Glenwood Springs. I admit I was a pill when I first got here.

I took them for granted, and I wasn't the easiest person to get along with. Thankfully, they forgave me. It's still unusual for me to have friends. I don't always know how to ask for help. I'm convinced, out of habit, that I should do everything on my own.

"Oh no, you don't!" I shout at the other poltergeist, winding up to throw a stapler through the window. She isn't floating too far above the ground, and I can reach it. She doesn't see me sneak up from behind as I wrench it from her hand.

When she realizes the stapler is gone, she spins around to face me. "Why you..." she scowls, searching for something else to throw at me. When she hurls a heavy book in my direction, I duck just in time.

Who knew ghost wrangling could be such a workout? After she grabs a sign off the wall, Juliet mutters a spell using a language I don't understand, but both poltergeists vanish in a poof of pink smoke.

"Whoa!" I exclaim. "How did you do that?"

"It's just a temporary vanishing spell. Emphasis on temporary. It may only last a few hours, but at least it will keep them quiet for a bit. Did I get everybody?" she asks.

"Yes!" I smile gratefully at her. "There were only two."

She twitches her shoulder like it was nothing. "I wish I could make it permanent. I can't believe there were only two, given the trouble they were causing."

With the flying objects stopped, at least for now, everyone left in the museum breathes a sigh of relief, stepping out from their hiding places.

"Thank you so much for your help, ladies!" Mr. Beasley exclaims.

"This should hold them for a while. But if I can't reason with them, we may need a professional medium to banish them permanently," I explain.

"How long would that take? I have a valuable doll coming from a collection in Denver late this afternoon. I don't want anything to happen to it," he tells me, worry etched in his face.

"I can perform a calming charm to surround the building that will keep things quiet for a bit longer," Wendy tells him. "But like Juliet's spell, it isn't permanent. Holly is right. I think you'll need a medium."

"I'd be grateful for anything you could do!" Mr. Beasley exclaims.

"What kind of doll is it?" I ask him, wondering how any doll could be worthy of so much fuss?

"Have you ever heard of the Bebe Mothereau collection?" he asks.

"Not once." I shake my head, along with Juliet and Wendy.

"That's a shame," Mr. Beasley *tsks*. "The signed copy I'm getting is quite rare. They were created in the 1800s by a French doll maker." He holds out his phone to show us a picture of the doll. We visibly cringe.

"That is one creepy-looking doll!" I exclaim.

He snatches the phone away, pressing it to his chest. "That creepy-looking doll is worth more than $20,000, Miss Daniel!"

Juliet and Wendy stare at him in shock. Naturally, I laugh. No way that doll is worth $20,000. Obviously, he's joking. But when he narrows his eyes at me in disgust, I realize he isn't.

"You're displaying a doll that's worth $20,000 *here*?"

"Yes! I'm selling tickets, which will bring in many visitors. Haven't you seen the posters around town advertising the event? That's why I must ensure the poltergeists are on their best behavior."

"Do you have enough security for a doll that valuable?" I ask, scanning the area for cameras, alarms, or at least bars on the windows.

"It's unnecessary," he waves his hand. "It's not the townspeople I'm worried about; it's the poltergeists."

"Seriously? You aren't worried about someone stealing the doll? Someone who knows how valuable it is?" This blows my mind. A $20,000 doll coming to this little museum, and his major concern is ghosts?

The Glenwood Doll Museum is near the train station. It's a small, red brick building with a flat roof. I was disappointed the first time I saw it. I was so sure a doll museum would resemble a dollhouse. How could it not?

Inside the museum are dolls of varying shapes, sizes, colors, and ages. Some are downright bizarre. I'm half-convinced they come to life when no one is around. A handful are displayed in doll houses, while others are perched on stands, seated in miniature chairs, or artfully arranged on a shelf.

Mr. Beasley, the museum owner, is a squatty little man with curly gray hair and small, square glasses. I still don't understand why Sheriff Mack laughed when he heard the name, after I announced I was becoming a Paranormal Private Investigator and Mr. Beasley was a client.

Even more shocking, however, was the revelation that the sheriff could laugh. None of us knew what to do when the sound came out of him. I think I saw him smile once before that.

"You're new here, aren't you?" Mr. Beasley asks.

"Uh, well, yes, but what does that have to do with your store security?"

"I trust this town!" he insists.

"Okay." I shrug. Not my monkey, not my circus, I guess. He hired me to deal with poltergeists, not to ensure that a valuable doll isn't stolen, so I'll just shut my mouth and be on my way.

"Remember, the calming charm along with the disappearing spell are temporary. The poltergeists will be back," Wendy reminds him.

"Why don't I come back tomorrow, before you open. I'll see if I can reason with the poltergeists. I'll let you know then if you should take additional action to eradicate them."

"That sounds like a fine plan!" Mr. Beasley exclaims. "I'll see you tomorrow."

On our way out the door, Wendy pulls me aside whispering, "Watch your back, okay, Holly?" she says in an unusually ominous tone.

"Why?"

"I have a bad feeling about this one."

I regard her thoughtfully. "A bad feeling Wendy-style or bad feeling witchy-premonition-style?"

"The second one." She sighs.

"Uh oh. That's serious. What do you mean, bad?"

"I'm not sure because I don't have a clear picture yet, but it's dark. This museum has a reputation for dark energy which the poltergeists feed on. Just be careful, okay?"

"Okay. I'm sure I'll be fine, but I'll be extra careful." I know better than to ignore her premonitions.

After we say our goodbyes, and I repeatedly swear to watch my six, I climb into my shockingly pink, fully restored VW Bus.

"How did it go? Did you give those old poltergeists the what for?" Clara, my 143-year-old flannel nightgown-wearing roommate, asks while air boxing pretend ghosts. "Pow! Pow! Pow!" she exclaims dramatically. She loves to watch old Batman reruns on tv.

"Poltergeists are nasty!" Mystery exclaims from the back seat, pursing her lips in disgust before licking her paw. She rubs it along her ear as if the mere thought of a poltergeist leaves her unkempt.

Mystery is my other roommate. A talking ghost cat whose age is unknown. She's a large, beautiful gray and white striped cat with fluffy ears. The first time she talked to me, I was so shocked I had to sit down. She and Clara still find it hilarious.

"These spirits aren't leaving anytime soon," I explain, "but Wendy temporarily banned them so we could get the visitors out. Mr. Beasley told me he's expecting an expensive collectible doll this afternoon, so Juliet enacted a calming charm which will buy us some time. I'll continue to negotiate with the poltergeists Otherwise, I'll call in a medium to remove them."

Wendy waves at us while leaving the parking lot on her mint green Vespa scooter. She styles her hair in a trendy faux hawk.

Today it's magenta with black stripes. The first time I met her, it was varying shades of blue.

The tattoos that cover her arms feature book-related quotes and pictures. She owns the used bookstore on Maple and 6th St. called The Looking Glass, and it's the coziest place I've ever visited. Her personality is as colorful as her hair and her tattoos. Clara and I wave back. While Wendy can't see her, she knows she's there.

Juliet pulls up to the VW before leaving. "Promise me you'll be careful!" she shouts. She's the nurturing mother figure in our group who owns Sol Conceptions, a bakery on Grand Avenue where I consume far too many calories.

They're delicious calories for sure, even so, I indulge in the delightful homemade sweets more than I should. Her big brown eyes gaze up at me through her turquoise cat glasses, daring me to defy her.

"I promise!" I call back.

"Tell her I said hello!" Clara urges, squeezing my arm with her icy hand.

"Clara says hi."

"Hi, Clara!" Juliet waves back.

"Humans," Mystery groans rolling her green feline eyes.

2

"**C**an we visit the drive-through? Please!" Clara begs when I pull out of the parking lot.

"I don't understand why you like the drive-through so much. It's not like anyone can see you," I patiently remind her.

"It's such a modern invention, though. For me anyway. When I was a little girl, we had drive *ins*, but I get such a kick out of watching you order through the speaker."

"Fine," I concede.

"Yay!" Clara claps her hands, bouncing up and down in the passenger seat.

I won't admit it to them, but I have trouble saying no to my roommates. If they knew the truth, I'd never get a moment's peace. I pretend that using the coffee shop drive-through is a hassle, but I secretly enjoy their happiness.

"I'll take a catppacino, please!" Mystery tells me from the back seat.

"Of course, you will," I nod.

I pull into the drive-through at the It's Bean A Delight Coffee Shop. I order a matcha latte for me, a bubble tea for Clara, and a catppacino for Mystery.

The cashier hands me our drinks while I place Mystery's treat on the back seat reminding her not to spill because I don't want to clean whipped cream off the seats again.

Next, I put Clara's bubble tea in the custom drink holder I installed at her request. It sits at just the right level for her to sip her drink from a straw, because while she can move small objects and close doors, she can't hold a cup for an extended period.

Not that she actually needs to drink anything. She just thinks it's fun. A year ago, I was living in Florida and pretending I couldn't see ghosts. If you told me this is what my life would become, I wouldn't have believed you. Not even for a moment. While I wouldn't have purposely chosen to share my home with two ghosts, they're good company, just quirky enough to be fun.

I bend the straw, so it sits at just the right level for her. "How is that?" I ask.

"Perfect!" she exclaims, giving me the thumbs up.

When I swivel back around to pay for our drinks, I laugh at the cashier's expression.

"Don't ask!" I tell her, waving my hand through the air like I do this all the time, which I do.

I pull into a parking spot then tune the car radio to our favorite classic rock station while we settle in to enjoy our treats.

While we're relaxing, a voice says, "Do you realize I saw that VW at least three blocks away?"

I turn to see Sheriff Mack, my arch-nemesis, standing next to the bus.

"Good afternoon, Sheriff," I tell him.

Part of me can't stand the guy, while the other part secretly enjoys our back and forth. He's no fan of my work as a Paranormal Private Investigator, yet when I was trying to secure my Private Investigator's license, and the paperwork got lost at the county office, he called in a favor with them and fast-tracked a new application.

He's a tall, imposing man who takes full advantage of his intimidating stature and consistently crisp uniform. I've noticed he rarely smiles. Instead, he always sports this perma-stern, no-nonsense expression. Helpful for making suspects wither, no doubt.

"Is Clara with you?" he asks.

I nod my head while sipping my latte.

"Hi, Clara," he says, peering into the back seat.

"She's in the passenger seat." I gesture with my thumb in her direction.

"Good afternoon, Sheriff!" she exclaims, beaming at him.

"She says good afternoon," I tell him.

Then he nods at the bus. "This thing running, okay?"

Is that a guy thing? To ask how well one's car is operating? Their version of *where did you get those shoes?*

"I guess so." I shrug. How am I supposed to know? If it gets me from one place to another, I assume it's running well. Although that may be how I ended up with a gazillion miles on my Subaru before it finally died while parked at the Red Castle Hotel where I tend bar on the side.

"You remind me of Scooby Doo. Solving mysteries in your VW bus."

Is Sheriff Mack referencing a beloved *cartoon*? Is he making a joke? I almost don't know what to say. I'm so stunned.

"You're a fan of Scooby Doo?" I ask.

"Who isn't?" he smiles.

"You know, your face is so much more pleasant when you smile. You should do it more often."

Ack! Did I seriously just say that to him? I'm a horrible person. I didn't mean it like that. What I'm really thinking is that he's attractive when he smiles, but I'll never admit it. Instead, I blurt out something that makes me sound like a jerk.

"You'd have more friends if you weren't so unpleasant," he tells me with a tip of his hat, then off he goes.

Ouch! I guess I deserved that. I twist around to Clara, who's suddenly obsessed with the tapioca balls in her drink. "I have plenty of friends, don't I?"

Clara nods her head vigorously. Then she plays with her drink some more. I guess that's all I'm getting out of her.

3

We drive home after our pit stop. While everyone we pass waves at us. I swear I feel like a homecoming queen on a parade float when that happens. It's the pink VW.

In the beginning, I thought it was ridiculous. I refused to wave back while vowing to paint it a different color. I was thinking of a basic beige so it would blend in. No one would wave at a beige bus after all.

However, as the town grew on me, I waved back. Little kids get so excited. They pump their arms to signal that I should honk the horn. Clara is trying to convince me to install a horn she found online that plays Batman-themed music. I told her she's pushing her luck.

Sheriff Mack insists he can see the bus three blocks away. He's wrong. They can see this thing from the International Space Station.

No, I didn't pick this car on purpose; rather, it chose me. On my first day in Glenwood Springs, Clara correctly predicted that the noise my old Subbie was making meant it wasn't long for this world.

I scoffed at her.

It died the next day.

Weirdly, the previous owners left behind this painfully bright pink, fully restored 1960 Volkswagen Bus. I instantly hated it. But it was a free car, so why not drive it?

Why did they leave it behind? They thought it was haunted. Technically, it is. It has a pink-flannel-nighty-wearing ghost in it. Although they can't leave the property under their own power, for reasons unbeknownst to Clara and Mystery, they can ride in the VW. Now that they live with someone who can see them, they pester me non-stop for car rides.

After my husband was killed serving the US Army in Iraq, I sold our house in Florida, collected his life insurance check, along with my severance check from my job (I had a bit of a temper problem back then), and moved to a sleepy little mountain town in Colorado known as Glenwood Springs.

I found this gorgeous house for a steal. But of course, at that price, it came with a catch. It's haunted.

I still say they should be required to disclose that part when selling. *I* didn't even realize it was haunted until the day I moved in. The sellers told people in town they were sure there were multiple ghosts, but it's just Clara and Mystery. Clara takes pride in the fact she caused so much trouble they thought there were several of her.

The house truly is amazing. There's a spacious wraparound porch where we love to spend our afternoons hanging out and drinking iced tea while listening to the Colorado River flowing nearby.

Inside, the architecture is original, with hardwood floors and stairs that creak when I climb them. The kitchen has a gas stove which I'm sure would be awesome if I knew how to cook. I should learn.

Not only did I never imagine myself living with ghosts, I certainly didn't picture myself as a Paranormal Private Investigator, but it's what I do now. Yes, I see dead people.

My parents recognized my gift long ago when I was about six years old, after my friend's grandma died. We took a casserole to their house, and I shocked them when they discovered me in the backyard engaged in a spirited discussion with the recently deceased.

They initially thought it was an imaginary friend, but then they knew she was real when grandma told me about the shoebox full of money she had stashed under a loose floorboard in the attic.

It was perfectly logical to me. Grandma said she couldn't enter the light until she told someone about the money. I wasn't even scared. It was fun having her to myself when the adults at the wake were busy talking to each other.

When it kept happening, though, my parents realized I had a special talent. Thankfully, they accepted my gift with open hearts but were concerned others wouldn't be so tolerant. They also worried that those who weren't afraid of me would try to exploit me.

They died when I was ten years old, so the state placed me in foster care. I knew instinctively that I had to hide what I could do. The system is hard enough *without* having paranormal talents. The few times I got caught, the other kids picked on me relentlessly. They also thought I was talking to imaginary friends.

I was always an outsider, as a foster kid, anyway. I bounced from home to home, so I changed schools a lot. Foster parents never had much money to spend on us, so I wore hand-me-down, worn-out clothes.

Kids are mean. I learned the hard way they'll readily exploit anyone who's even slightly different. I was lonely, The few times I let my guard down to talk to a spirit and got caught, I instantly regretted it. My lavender eyes already convinced them I was a witch. My conversations with thin air had them accusing me of inventing imaginary friends.

Eventually, I honed my ability to ignore the ghosts completely. I hid it so well that even my husband Ben never knew about it. I always planned to tell him - someday. But then the Casualty Notification Officer showed up on my doorstep at 5:37 AM on a Tuesday and *someday* became never.

It's not as easy as you might think to hide it. I've had ghosts confront me at grocery stores and movie theaters. I ignore them, but some get downright belligerent. They get in my face and yell at me.

When I applied to work as a bartender at the Red Castle Hotel here in Glenwood Springs, a ghost knocked a Glencairn glass off the bar because I wouldn't acknowledge him.

I lost my temper and yelled at him in front of the hotel manager. Despite my vehement denial, the manager knew immediately what I was doing. He begged me to help him locate a missing tiara with the help of the hotel ghosts.

Now I'm a Paranormal Private Investigator. I don't just solve paranormal mysteries, though. Most are a combination of the paranormal and your standard everyday mystery involving misbehaving humans.

Most recently, I helped a woman find her lost wedding ring. The ghost living in their house saw the cat push it off the dresser, where it fell into the heating vent. I didn't tell her the cat did it. But I advised her to put it inside her jewelry box whenever she takes it off from now on.

It was one of my easier jobs but seeing the excitement in her eyes and experiencing the gratitude gave me the warm fuzzies. After my previous work in the pressure cooker, that is cybersecurity, I'm so much more relaxed and happier now.

I still tend bar at the Red Castle Hotel occasionally. I enjoy mixing drinks, chatting with the guests, and swapping stories with the spirits who live there. Upon moving to Glenwood, I discovered Wendy's used bookstore and Juliet's bakery.

Aside from my husband, Clara, Mystery, Juliet, and Wendy are the first genuine friends I've ever had. Admittedly, I don't always know how one should behave around friends.

While many of my previous acquaintances found it easier to tiptoe around me, hoping not to set me off, my friends here call me out on my destructive behavior. On multiple occasions, I've had to apologize to them for being selfish and brittle, but thankfully, they forgave me.

I had what I guess you could call friends when I lived in Florida, but those were work friends. The atmosphere was so competitive that they were mostly just people I got along with because I had to. I never even considered telling them I'm a spirit communicator.

I was shocked to learn that most citizens of Glenwood are rather laid back regarding the paranormal. Everyone knows the Red Castle Hotel is haunted. Tourists even come here hoping for a ghostly encounter.

Stories of ghostly sightings abound. Some are true. Most are highly exaggerated to add drama. However, I can confirm that it *is* haunted. I talk to ghosts a lot when I'm working in the bar.

However, my latest assignment at the museum has been particularly challenging. Poltergeists are new to me. I've encountered a few of them in the past, but this is the first time I've attempted to work with them. I'm worried that someone will get hurt as their poor behavior escalates.

I hope that when I talk to them tomorrow, I can persuade them to dial back the severe pranks or even go somewhere else. I'm convinced that the two I saw today are feeding off a specific dark energy presence. I can determine what that is, then perhaps I'll get them to settle down. Unfortunately, that could take more than just a day's worth of talking, though.

I devote the rest of my afternoon to studying some of the dusty, yellow-paged books on poltergeists that Wendy found for me at an estate sale.

I'm so lost in my work that I almost miss my usual lap time at the hot springs.

"I'm going to the pool, Clara!" I shout on my way out the door.

"If you see Renaldo tell him he still owes me $5 from our bet last month!" she calls back.

"Will do!"

Renaldo is a ghost who drowned one night many years ago after getting drunk and sneaking into the pool after hours. How or why, Clara managed to place a bet with him is beyond me, but I'm learning to just nod my head and go along with these strange things.

The first time I saw Renaldo, I was swimming laps. Suddenly, there he was, waving and shouting at me with great excitement. For someone who constantly sees ghosts, it was still unnerving to come across one underwater.

I was so shocked I swallowed a bunch of water. I came up spluttering and choking so badly that a lifeguard rushed over, convinced I was drowning. Between reassuring the lifeguard that I was okay and dealing with Renaldo, who was firing questions at me simultaneously, I'm lucky they let me come back.

4

My leaden arms drag through the water while swimming my final laps for the evening. Dreams of a thick, melt-in-my-mouth donut topped with colorful frosting and bright sprinkles dance in my head. You know, the kind you can just sink your teeth into, savoring the fried, sugary goodness.

Ugh. Working out is hard enough without thinking of the pastry I'd rather be eating. Just two more laps, I promise myself. I know two more laps doesn't sound like much, but in a pool this size, it's an eternity. There are two pools here and one of them spans over 400 feet long.

It's so long that they've placed the lap lanes across the width instead of lengthwise, like most pools do. Yet even the width is 100 feet long, which makes it a vigorous workout. Then, after swimming so many laps, I still must make my way to the end of the monstrously long pool, exhausting me even further.

The first time I saw the pools, I was standing on the pedestrian bridge spanning the I-70 highway and the Colorado River, surrounded by jagged mountain peaks pointing to the heavens. It took my breath away. The pools are longer than two city blocks! How could they possibly be that big?

Sure, I saw them on the internet and read about them in travel brochures, but that was nothing compared to seeing them in person. Along with the haunted hotels, the hot springs draw travelers from around the world. Tourists have enjoyed the pools' 15-mineral-infused healing waters since the late 1800s.

They're geothermally heated, so they're open year-round. I secretly want to visit them on Christmas Eve, in the snow, while watching the sun set behind the mountains. For now, I try to swim laps at least three days a week in the evenings.

I do this so I can eat the delightful pastries Juliet sells in her bakery. It's also relaxing simply to float around in the warm, nurturing waters. I think of it as a giant bathtub without the bubbles. But how cool would that be? Bubbles! I wonder if anyone else has thought of that.

By the time I'm done for the evening, it's 9 PM. The lifeguards are kicking everyone out. I shower and head out to the parking lot, still fantasizing about sugary donuts.

The $20,000 doll and pair of poltergeists are also still on my mind. I'll drive past the museum, hoping I might catch Mr. Beasley hard at work so we can discuss the situation further.

When I pull into the parking lot, I'm surprised to see every light inside the building on with the front door wide open. His car is still here, so he must be working. Maybe the door is open because he had to carry something inside.

At least it's a good excuse to stick my head in the door and say hello. I tiptoe into the museum - I don't want to startle Mr. Beasley unnecessarily. I'm sure he's on edge with the poltergeists and expensive doll as it is.

"Hello! Mr. Beasley?" I call out, gently tapping on the door. "I saw the lights on and figured it was okay to stop by! Hello?" I'm almost afraid to see the creepy doll.

I spy a prominent display that wasn't here earlier. The tag reads *Signed Bebe Mothereau 1883*, but there's no doll. Maybe it was delayed.

Or Mr. Beasley might be in the back preparing it. I'm relieved that Wendy and Juliet's spells must still be in place because there's no sign of the poltergeists.

When I hear the back door slam shut, I call his name again. I jokingly think to myself that perhaps the creepy doll broke free and is now wandering Glenwood Springs, terrorizing the residents. Not that dolls can actually do that. At least, I don't think so.

I'm so distracted by my morbid doll thoughts, though, that by the time I realize there's a large, heavy glass box on the floor, it's too late, and I trip. I fall hard, bruising my hands and knees in the process and possibly a rib.

The fall knocks the wind out of me. I struggle to catch my breath, but not before I swear several times at my clumsiness. When I spot a pair of shoes in front of me I scream.

5

A pair of feet, mere inches from my face, peeks out from under the massive bookcase where the elderly couple was hiding just a few hours before. The person under the overturned bookshelf must be dead. We are *not* in Kansas anymore! I mutter. I try to stand up, but it's painful. I hope I didn't break any bones.

"Mr. Beasley?" I whisper. I recognize the shoes from earlier, so I know it's him. I have to get the bookshelf off him! I also need to call 911. But if there's a chance, he's still alive...

What if he's under there struggling to breathe? I try desperately to lift the shelf, but it's even heavier than I thought. I can't budge it. Not even a little.

"Freeze! Sheriff!".

I pause mid-lift.

"Put your hands in the air and stand up slowly!"

I do as I'm told.

"Now turn around and face me. *Slowly*."

I turn around.

"Ms. Daniel," Sheriff Mack says icily, after I turn around.

"You've had lunch at my house, Sheriff. I think you can call me Holly." Why did I say that? Why do I always say such dumb things to him?

The deputy's eyebrow shoots up , glancing at the sheriff. "Should I cuff her?" he asks, turning to the sheriff.

"No. Not at the moment, anyway," he grunts.

When they re-holster their guns, I drop my hands. "What happened here?" Sheriff Mack asks. When I realize they haven't seen him yet, I point to Mr. Beasley's feet.

"Hands up!" the deputy shouts. I throw my hands in the air again.

"Move!" Sheriff Mack yells as I jump out of the way. He lunges toward the bookcase.

"Help me lift this!" he barks at his deputy, while re-holstering his gun. They struggle to lift the bookshelf. When they get it upright, we cringe at seeing Mr. Beasley's crushed body underneath. Yuck. Sheriff Mack radios for backup while the deputy tells me to put my hands behind my back. Is he handcuffing me.

"Wait, you think I did this?" I squeak.

"We caught you kneeling over the body," he points out.

"I just got here!" I insist.

"It looks like you were in a struggle." He gestures to my bruises.

"I fell over that." I point at the glass box on the floor. My throat is suddenly parched. My voice higher pitched than normal. How could he think I did this? I keep glancing at Sheriff Mack, but he's on the phone and doesn't notice my distress.

The deputy throws a look over his shoulder at the glass box. "Nice excuse," he sneers.

"What were you doing here after hours?" Sheriff Mack asks, now that he's off the phone. "You don't strike me as the doll type."

"I told you at my house that the doll museum was a new client!"

He nods his head while the deputy turns to him again. "What do you mean, client?" he asks.

I'm at a momentary loss for words. It's still uncomfortable for me to admit I see dead people. It's easier than it used to be, but it feels unnatural.

"She's a Paranormal Private Investigator," Sheriff Mack says, rolling his eyes.

"What's that?" the deputy asks.

"I see dead people," I finally admit.

"Nuh-uh!" he exclaims, whirling back and forth between the sheriff and me. He probably thinks he's in the middle of some weird reality tv show.

"It's true," the sheriff interjects. "She talks to ghosts. Hey, is this display missing its doll?" he looks around for the missing collectible.

"It's a $20,000 doll on loan from a collector in Denver," I explain.

"So, where is it?" he asks again.

"I don't know. Mr. Beasley told me earlier that it was supposed to arrive this afternoon. But I didn't see it when I walked in just now."

"Were you here to steal it?" the deputy asks.

"What? No!" First, they think I killed a man. Now they think I stole a $20,000 doll?

"Then why were you here?"

"Do I need a lawyer?" I ask, gesturing with my hands still cuffed behind me.

"I don't know, do you?" the deputy fires back.

I squint at him using my best mean girl glare. "I thought they only said that on tv."

The deputy's cheeks color while Sheriff Mack swivels away to keep from laughing. Too late. I caught the smirk on his face, even if the deputy didn't.

"Where were you before you got here?" Sheriff Mack asks.

"I was swimming laps at the pool."

The deputy leans in to sniff my hair, and I step back. I would have swatted at him if my hands weren't bound.

"Doesn't smell like sulfur," he says.

"I took a shower!" I retort.

By then, the Medical Examiner's office and several additional investigators arrive. They see the body, stare at me with the handcuffs, and sneer.

"I didn't do it!" I insist.

They ignore me as they unpack and set up their equipment. I'm sure they hear that constantly, but in this case, it's true.

"Can someone get these off me?" I gesture at the handcuffs again while they ignore me.

"Do you have a time of death?" Sheriff Mack asks the ME.

"Couldn't have been more than an hour ago. If that," he explains, removing the thermometer from Mr. Beasley's body.

"Is there anyone who can vouch for you at the pool this evening?" the deputy asks.

I think back to the conversation I had with Renaldo while I was swimming laps.

"He means living," Sheriff Mack snaps at me while the others seem confused about why he had to clarify the question.

"I guess the girl I showed my pass to at the desk," I shrug.

"Does this girl have a name?" the sheriff asks.

"Ashley?"

"Are you asking me or telling me?" Sheriff Mack asks.

"I'm not sure of her name!" I grumble. Why must he be so frustrating?

"Write down her description," he says, thrusting his notepad in my direction while I stare at him.

"Uncuff, her deputy," he sighs.

"Are you sure?" the deputy says.

"Yes!"

The deputy removes the handcuffs, while I take the notepad from the sheriff to write out Ashley's, or whatever her name is, description.

"Oh! Hey! I just remembered that when I first got here, I heard the backdoor slam shut," I mention hopefully.

"Likely story," the ME mutters. Great. Everybody thinks I'm guilty.

"What were you doing here again?" Sheriff Mack asks.

"I told you, he's a client."

"You always visit your clients at 10 PM?" he presses.

"No, not usually, but I stopped this evening after swimming because I was curious about the doll." I start to explain that Mr. Beasley hired me to deal with unruly poltergeists but think better of it as everyone pauses their work to listen.

"Should I arrest her?" the deputy asks.

"Not at this time." Sheriff Mack says while I breathe a sigh of relief. "But don't leave town and be prepared to answer additional questions at a moment's notice, got it?"

I seriously consider saying something rude but think better of it. The old me would have lost my temper and gotten myself into even more trouble than I already am.

"Not a problem," I respond quickly. "Can I go now?" I ask, thrusting the notebook back into the sheriff's hands.

"Yes, you can go," he says, pausing for a moment. "But touch nothing on the way out. Go straight home. I'm sure we'll have more questions for you tomorrow."

"Aye aye, Sheriff!" I give him a stiff salute. But when he glares at me, I wonder again why I say such cringeworthy things in front of him.

I rush around the yellow crime scene tape and out the door before any of them change their minds.

Pausing outside the museum I breathe in the heavy summer night air that carries a hint of sulfur from the pools. I'm still in a daze. I can't believe Mr. Beasley is dead.

Sheriff Mack can't seriously think I did this, can he? Is it rude to wish Beasley's spirit had stuck around to tell me who did this to him? It would certainly make my life easier.

Of course, I feel horrible that he died. I'd also like to know who could have done such a thing. My head swims as I drop down on the edge of the museum walkway just to take a break. I'm not sure I can drive at this point. My emotions weigh heavily on me.

There are at least a half dozen cop cars in the museum parking lot, with their red and blue lights flashing in the dark. I stare absent mindedly at the sign that reads Glenwood Doll Museum. Despite the warm evening, I shiver. The flashing lights bounce off the sign, further hypnotizing me.

"Why so glum, chum?" a spirit appears so suddenly, it makes me jump.

"I just found out someone I know, a client, was killed tonight. The sheriff thinks I had something to do with it."

"Did you?" she asks.

"No!" I respond angrily.

It's hard to see her clearly. While the police car lights continue to illuminate the sign, they just stream through her. She's a young woman, probably in her 20s when she passed.

Her t-shirt and jeans could have come from nearly any modern era, but I'd say she died within the last few years. Her long, mousy brown hair hangs in her face.

Suddenly it occurs to me she may live here. Did she see something? "Hey, do you live here?" I ask.

But before she can answer, Juliet and Wendy call out for me. "Holly! Holly! Are you okay?"

She disappears in an instant as my friends argue with a deputy from the Sheriff's Department to let them cross the yellow tape barrier.

"It's okay, deputy, they're with me," I assure him as I approach them at the line. "What are you guys doing? How did you know I was here?" I ask.

"The sheriff called. He said you might need some help," Juliet explains.

I glance back at the museum as if that will explain which sheriff they're talking about. Surely it isn't Sheriff Mack.

"What sheriff?" I ask.

Wendy looks confused. "The only sheriff in town, Sheriff Mack," she reminds me.

"*My* Sheriff Mack?" I point to myself. "I mean, *our* Sheriff Mack?"

"Well, yes," Juliet responds, even more confused than Wendy.

Well, what do you know? Maybe he doesn't hate me after all.

"What happened? Are you hurt? Why are the cops here?" Juliet asks, checking me over for any blood.

"Why are you bruised and dirty?" Wendy adds.

I scrutinize my purple knees and t-shirt with dirt streaks on it from falling on the floor. It does appear that I've been in a scuffle—no wonder the deputy wanted to haul me down to the station.

I quickly pull Wendy and Juliet aside, so we're out of earshot from the deputy guarding the yellow tape line.

"Mr. Beasley is dead. Sheriff Mack thinks I killed him!" I whisper dramatically.

"Mr. Beasley is dead?" Wendy covers her mouth but not before a sob escapes.

"The sheriff thinks you killed him?" Juliet asks, equally dismayed.

"They put handcuffs on me!" I explain miserably.

"What happened?" Juliet asks. "How did he die?"

"Someone pushed a heavy bookcase on him and crushed him!"

My friends cringe.

"Believe me, whatever you're imagining, it was far worse in person." I shudder.

"Who could have done such a thing?" Wendy cries.

"It certainly wasn't me!"

"We know that honey," Juliet says, resting a reassuring hand on my shoulder. It's nice to have them here with me. I suppose I should thank the sheriff for calling them, although I'm still mad at him for even entertaining the possibility that I could have done such a thing. Even if they did find me in the museum, after hours, standing over the body.

When the news station truck pulls up to the museum, Juliet and Wendy each take an arm pulling me away from the scene.

"Let's get you home," Juliet tells me. "We don't need to be around here with the reporters."

"But my bus is still here," I point back to my VW sitting there looking forlorn, alone in the parking lot. Meanwhile, the investigators comb through Mr. Beasley's car as we speak.

"I don't think you should drive right now. We'll take you home. You can get that pink monstrosity tomorrow," Juliet explains in that steady, reassuring voice that I've come to count on.

"Okay, maybe you're right," I say with one last glance back at my pink bus. How odd that tonight I regard it fondly when only last month I wanted to get rid of it.

6

C lara is waiting for us on the porch, concern etched across her face. "Where have you been? Are you okay? Is it true? Mr. Beasley is dead, and you're a suspect?" she cries, wringing her luminescent hands.

"I'm not a suspect. I'm a person of interest," I protest. Yes, that sounds so much better. "Hang on. Who says I'm a suspect?" How does she know about Mr. Beasley already?

"It's on the news. Mystery and I were binge-watching the Good Witch when we saw everything on tv."

"Oh great," I groan. "They've already announced that I'm a person of interest?"

We file into the house while Clara points at the tv. There's a video feed of Wendy and Juliet leading me away from the crime scene while a young, blonde reporter with big hair narrates in the background.

"The Sheriff's Department has identified a Ms. Holly Daniel as a person of interest in this horrific crime. Ms. Daniel is a newcomer to the Glenwood Springs area and works part-time as a bartender at the Red Castle Hotel.

"You may recall that she was involved in the recent theft of Lucy M's stolen tiara..." she drones on. "Authorities have told us that along with the murder, a rare collectible doll worth at least $20,000 is missing and presumed stolen."

"Hey!" I exclaim. "I *solved* the tiara mystery! Why doesn't she include that part? These reporters are all alike. Who told them I'm a person of interest? I swear if it was Sheriff Mack..."

"Holly, calm down. Why don't you take a seat? Wendy will make you some of her calming tea. It's a special blend," Juliet croons, leading me to a chair, gently pushing me into it.

I wince when I lower myself into the comfy chair. The adrenalin is wearing off, and my bruises are noticeably worse.

"I have a healing salve I created the other day. I'll get it out of the car, and we'll fix you up," Juliet offers as Wendy hands me a cup of tea. One sip and I feel better already.

Have I mentioned that witch friends are incredibly convenient? When Juliet returns with the salve, I rub it on my bruises. It's a clear gel that smells faintly of mint and lavender. The pain subsides immediately while my muscles relax.

"It won't take away the pain completely, but it should help a lot," Juliet explains.

"It's helping already. Thank you. Both of you."

Clara and Mystery hover in front of me as I tell them what happened at the museum.

"Oh! I almost forgot!" I sit forward, eagerly. "Before you got there," I nod at Wendy and Juliet, "a ghost appeared while I was sitting on the curb. A young woman."

"Did she say anything?" Clara asks, excitedly.

"We didn't get the chance to really talk because she disappeared as soon as Wendy and Juliet showed up."

"You talk to ghosts every day," Juliet reminds me. "What's different about this one?"

"It just seems odd that she appeared at that moment, if you know what I mean."

"Does she live in the museum?" Mystery asks.

"She must," I shrug. "I wanted to question her more, hoping she saw something tonight, but then poof, she was gone."

"What about our friends, the poltergeists? Were they there?" Wendy asks.

I shake my head. "I didn't see them, so either they were hiding, or your spells are still working."

"Wouldn't a room full of law enforcement have been the perfect time to indulge in their shenanigans?" Juliet asks.

"I would think. Maybe your spells were still in place." I point out.

Wendy smacks her forehead with her hand. "I just realized if we hadn't used that sleeping spell, they could have been active and either prevented Mr. Beasley's death or at least been a witness to it," she groans. "Now I feel bad. What if we knocked them out too well?"

"How could you have known something like this would happen?" I offer.

"What if the poltergeists *did* it?" Wendy gasps.

"Killed Mr. Beasley?" I ask.

"I didn't think of that!" Juliet says, looking horrified. "It's possible, right?"

"From what I've been studying in Wendy's books, poltergeists *have* killed. Although it's unusual, it's not impossible."

"What about the stolen doll? Poltergeists wouldn't kill over a collector's doll, would they?" Clara asks.

"I don't think so."

"What if the doll did it?" Mystery suggests.

"What if the doll did what?" I ask.

"Killed Mr. Beasley!" she exclaims.

"Then ran off into the night?" I remember thinking that the doll could be on the run, and now I feel weird about it, even if I was joking at the time.

"I heard the back door slam shut right after I arrived," I add.

"See!" Mystery exclaims.

"It must have been the killer!" Wendy says. "You told the cops that, right?"

I nod my head. "I mentioned it, but no one took it seriously."

"They thought you were making an excuse," Clara says, while I nod my head again.

"I think you should go to bed," Wendy urges when she sees my eyelids droop, "we'll talk about this again in the morning."

"Maybe they'll find the murderer and the doll by then, and I won't have to worry about it anymore, right?"

Everyone nods their heads. They don't believe it will be that easy any more than I do.

7

The following morning I awake to Clara and Mystery peering into my face.

"Is she dead?" Mystery asks.

"I don't think so. Poor thing, she was exhausted." Clara fusses.

"How can we tell if she's dead?" Mystery says.

"I'm not dead!" I exclaim, startling them both.

"See there. She isn't dead!" Clara tells Mystery, folding her arms over her chest appearing triumphant.

"I didn't really think she was dead," Mystery says, rolling her eyes. She wanders off, her tail held high, swishing to and fro.

"Wendy's tea knocked me out," I murmur.

"I think you needed the sleep, dear," Clara says.

"Any news about Mr. Beasley's murder? Did they catch the killer yet?"

"The newspaper is on the porch, but I was waiting for you to get up," Clara informs me.

I know it seems weird that we get an actual newspaper. I wouldn't bother, but Clara likes to read it. Even though she spends a lot of time on the internet, she still enjoys the idea of getting her news from the Glenwood Gazette.

I'm surprised to discover I feel rather spry this morning. Juliet's salve must have done the trick. She should sell that stuff.

I shuffle down to the kitchen in my favorite robe and fuzzy rabbit slippers for some coffee. After I start the coffeemaker, I step onto the patio to get the newspaper.

I'm almost afraid to open it, but I can't put it off forever. I pull off the rubber band, unroll the paper, groaning in dismay when I see the front page. There's a picture of the museum on the left and an unflattering picture of me on the right. The headline reads, "Doll museum owner found dead; new resident listed as the only person of interest."

"Great. Just great," I mutter.

Clara gasps when she sees the story. "Where did they get that picture? It's horrible," she shakes her head.

She's right. They could have used a much better picture. Although, I imagine the unflattering picture may be the least of my concerns at this point. Announcing to the entire town that I'm the only person of interest in a murder and theft of a one-of-a-kind doll really should be my biggest worry.

I sip my piping hot cup of dark roast coffee while scanning the newspaper. The article doesn't tell me anything I don't already know. Mr. Beasley was found dead, and a rare doll is missing.

The reporter also talked to the person in Denver who owns it. He's furious. He's threatening to sue the museum if the doll doesn't turn up soon.

"When I find that doll, I find the murderer," I tell Clara. "I'm sure of it."

"So, you're officially investigating?" she asks eagerly.

"I still don't know." I hesitate.

"Hide! It's the popo again!" Mystery announces as she streaks through the kitchen.

I twist around in the chair to see Sheriff Mack approaching the porch. "Mystery, you really should stop calling him that!" I chastise. "Why are you always so worried? He can't even see you."

"Why does she do that?" I ask Clara.

"I think she just likes to be dramatic," she explains.

"Good morning, Sheriff," I tell him, opening the door.

"Good morning, Holly," he intones.

So now it's Holly, huh? I don't know if that makes me feel worthy or nervous.

"I'd ask you why you're here, but I think I already know." I hold up the newspaper. "Did *you* tell the reporter I'm a person of interest?"

He actually looks like he feels bad about it. Isn't that a surprise? "No, that wasn't me. It was Deputy Owens. I chewed him out afterward, in case you're wondering, but it was too late. It's already out there."

"Are you here to arrest me?" I ask almost jokingly, but then worry as soon as I say it. Maybe he really is here to arrest me. Would he at least let me change out of my bunny slippers into some shoes?

"I'm not arresting you. Not at the moment, anyway. I came to see if you remember anything more about last night. Anything that was out of place or unusual? Hey, is that fresh coffee I smell?" he pivots suddenly.

"It is. Would you like a cup?" I ask.

He hesitates. He probably shouldn't be asking a person of interest for coffee, but it's hard to pass up.

"Sure, why not," he says, removing his hat while following me to the kitchen.

"Have a seat. I'll get you a cup," I'll tell him.

When he nearly sits on Clara I bite my lip to keep from laughing. She dives out of the way but then happily stands at his elbow, looking him up and down.

"Isn't he smashing in his uniform?" she asks.

"Mmmm hmmm," I respond.

"What?" the sheriff asks.

"Clara wonders why you're here so early if you're not arresting me."

He looks around uncomfortably, as if Clara might suddenly appear and scare him.

"Cream or sugar?" I ask.

"Nope," he says.

Why am I not surprised?

"He even drinks his coffee like a real man," Clara swoons.

This time I don't respond out loud; I just gawk at her like that's possibly the weirdest thing I've ever heard.

"I know we didn't discuss this in detail last night, but why exactly were you at the museum when it was nearly 10:00?" he presses.

I explain everything that had happened earlier that day, before he saw us in the coffee shop parking lot, and what led me to stop at the museum after swimming.

"There's nothing additional that you can tell me? Any possible clue could really help your case here," he points out.

"Like I mentioned last night. Just as I walked into the museum, through the *unlocked* door I might add, I called Mr. Beasley's name. Then I heard the back door bang shut, so naturally, I thought it was him. But that's when I tripped over the glass display box and fell. Then you know the rest."

"You saw nothing, though?"

"Nope!"

"We think he originally placed the glass box over the doll as a display, so then whoever took the doll killed Mr. Beasley, pulled the glass box off the doll, dropped it on the floor, grabbed it, and ran. Possibly out the back door just as you arrived."

"So, it's obvious I didn't do it, right?" I'm feeling hopeful. Maybe this will be easier than I thought.

"It's not obvious to my people," he warns. "We caught you with your hands on the murder weapon. We also found your fingerprints in the museum."

"What? How can that be? How do you even have my fingerprints on file?"

"They fingerprinted you when you filed for your Private Investigator's license, remember?" he points out.

Oh yeah. "Of course, my fingerprints were there. I was in the museum earlier that day."

"I know that, and you know that, but..." he trails off.

"It still proves nothing," I sigh.

"I need to go now but thank you for the coffee. What I told you last night still stands. Don't leave town; I'm sure I'll need to question you again."

I nod my head sorrowfully. What a mess this is.

I escort him to the front door to see him out, but as I close it behind him, I recall he sent Wendy and Juliet to the crime scene last night when he knew I needed my friends.

"Hey, one more thing. I appreciate you sending my friends to the museum to pick me up last night."

He nods curtly, placing his hat back on his head.

"Nice slippers," he adds before walking away, but not before I catch just the slightest hint of what I'm sure is a smile.

8

— • —

"I 'll collect the bus and then decide what to do next," I tell Clara as Mystery emerges from behind the couch where she was hiding.

"You should have asked Sheriff Mack for a ride," Mystery suggests.

"I'm fine walking," I tell her.

Walking to the museum helps me ponder my next move. If the sheriff insists I'm a person of interest, then I don't have a choice. I must investigate this case.

I *am* a paranormal private investigator. This is kind of my job. Besides, how will I ever get new clients if people in this town think I killed one? Phew! The bus is still there, safe and sound.

I shudder just looking at the yellow crime scene tape surrounding the building. I peer into the windows to see if it looks any different from last night. Everything is pretty much as I saw it when I walked in.

"Hello!" the ghost from last night appears, startling me again.

"It's you!" I exclaim. "You disappeared on me last night."

"Crowds make me nervous," she gulps.

"But no one can see you," I point out.

"I just prefer it when everything is quiet."

"Okay, I get that. Do you live here?" I ask.

"Yep."

"You know the owner of the museum was murdered last night, right?"

"Yeah, I figured that out," she mumbles

"They think I did it," I tell her.

"That sucks. If you didn't do it, I bet it was one of those nasty poltergeists." She screws her face up like Mystery did when she said the same thing.

"You know the poltergeists?"

"Unfortunately, yes. They're disgusting," she exclaims.

"You sound like my cat. Hey, where were you when Mr. Beasley was killed? Did you see anything? I'm desperate here."

"I didn't see anyone except you. I think your VW is really sick, by the way."

"Oh, uh, thanks," I respond.

"Then I saw the police," she adds.

"I swear I didn't kill Mr. Beasley," I tell her.

"Whatever you say," she shrugs. "I believe you."

"Did you see anyone else here before me?" I ask desperately.

"I saw Mr. Beasley."

"No, aside from him. Or me. I swear I heard the back door close when I walked in," I explain.

"Oh, you know, I think I saw a man running away," she adds.

"You did? Can you describe him?" Please have a good description, I think to myself.

"It was dark, so I don't know."

"But you're sure it was a man," I press.

"I think so. I can't be certain, though. Maybe if you come back later, I could remember more..." she trails off.

Great. A lonely ghost who just wants someone to talk to. Which I can totally relate to, but right now, I want to find out who killed Mr. Beasley.

"Okay, I could come back later. What's your name, by the way?"

"I'm Bianca Posei," she says proudly.

"Good to meet you. I'm Holly Daniel."

"I know who you are," she nods her head. "Everyone in the Glenwood spirit community knows you. Most of us have never met a spirit communicator."

"I'll come back another time, so we can talk more," I assure her.

"Okay!" she exclaims.

I feel bad that she looks so happy at the thought of talking to me again. I remember what it's like to be lonely.

"Are your parents still alive?" I ask as delicately as possible. She can't be older than her early 20s at the most.

"I never knew my dad," she admits.

"How come?" I ask.

"He took off as soon as he found out my mom was pregnant."

"That's too bad."

"Who needs him?" She scrunches her face. "We were always poor. My mom worked two jobs to support us. She died from pneumonia when I was 15."

"I'm sorry about that. My parents died when I was ten, so I understand. Were you in foster care, too?"

"No."

"That's good. You had relatives who took you in?" I ask.

"Sometimes I think I would have been better off in the system," she tells me.

"Why?"

"They sent me to live with my aunt and uncle, who weren't happy about having another mouth to feed."

"Oh, that's too bad. Do you mind if I ask how you died? You seem awfully young," I point out.

"I ran with a bad crowd. I drank and partied too much. I got on the back of my boyfriend's motorcycle one night when he was drunk, and that's all I remember." She pauses as if this time the answer might come to her.

"Well, it was good talking to you, but I have several errands I have to run today, so I should be on my way," I tell her reluctantly.

"You'll come back, right?" she begs.

"Yes, absolutely."

On my way back to the bus I spot a small shoe on the ground. What the heck? It's too small for a baby's shoe, but it could fit a doll.

"Hey, do you know--?" I spin around, holding the shoe in the air for Bianca to see. Rats. Where did she go? Where did this come from? Could it be a clue, or did Mr. Beasley drop it earlier by mistake?

Maybe a child visiting the museum with their own doll dropped it. Or what if it's evidence? Then why didn't the cops see it last night? It was dark, and most of the action happened inside the museum.

Maybe they didn't see it? Or saw it but decided it was useless? I stuff it in my pocket. It's probably nothing, but you never know.

9

On my way to the bakery where Wendy and Juliet are waiting to discuss our options, I mentally tick off the facts we know. So far, I have a missing doll, a murdered museum owner, and no suspects. Plus, a Sheriff's Department that thinks I committed both crimes.

I'm annoyed to see all the parking spots in front of Juliet's bakery are taken, so I park down the street. As I was driving, I noticed very few people waved at me. Maybe I'm extra sensitive right now, but I swear they saw me then turned away.

What if they saw the news on tv, in addition to the awful picture in the newspaper. Yes, that still bothers me. If they're going to publish a picture of me, the least they could do is use a decent one, don't you think?

They can't seriously believe I would kill anyone. Yet walking to the bakery, I catch people staring and whispering. Others turn and walk in the opposite direction. Now I know something is up. If I don't sort this out, I'll either get arrested for murder or run out of town.

Even though my expertise is in spirit communication and bartending, I fear it's up to me to solve this, just like the stolen tiara.

"Hi, ladies!" I call out.

"Holly! It's so good to see you. How did you sleep?" Wendy asks, running up to me and giving me one of her famous hugs. Everyone knows her for her comforting hugs and special teas.

"We were worried when we didn't hear from you this morning," Juliet says.

I sigh. "It's been an interesting morning already. First Sheriff Mack stopped at my house--"

"What?" Wendy shrieks, her eyes blazing. "Is he harassing you? How could he think you'd kill Mr. Beasley? He didn't arrest you, did he? Were you in jail this morning? Why didn't you call us?"

"Calm down," I reassure her, holding my hands up hoping to ward off her incoming rant.

"Take a breath there, Miss Wendy," Juliet adds, patting her shoulder.

"He just wanted to ask me some more questions. He was hoping I remembered something new from last night," I reassure her.

"Did he tell the reporter you were a person of interest?" Juliet asks. "If he did, I'll be madder than a puffed toad."

I can always tell when Juliet is extra wound up because her southern upbringing shows through. Despite her urging Wendy to remain calm, *her* expression is now one of pure fire.

"No, he says the deputy did it," I tell them.

"That's just rude!" she responds.

"So, what took you so long to get here?" Wendy asks.

"I walked to the museum to pick up the bus." I hold up my hand to stop them from complaining. "I wanted the exercise," I quickly add; before either could protest, I didn't call them for a ride. "But it's good I did because I saw the ghost from last night again."

"The young woman?" Juliet asks.

"Yes."

"Did she see the killer?" Wendy jumps in.

"I'm not so sure." I wiggle my hand. "When I first asked, she said she saw nothing because she was in the parking lot. Supposedly, our poltergeist friends chased her from the museum."

"So, the poltergeists *were* active last night?" Juliet asks, her eyes wide with surprise.

"According to her, yes."

"What do you mean when you *first asked,* she said she saw nothing?" Wendy questions.

"After I told her I heard the back door slam shut, she remembered she saw a man running away."

"What did he look like?" Juliet asks.

"She says she didn't get a good view of him. But I'm uncertain that she actually saw someone. She said she'd talk to me about it if I returned later."

Wendy scrunches her face. "I'm confused; why would she say she did if she didn't?"

"I think she's lonely and wants a friend. The poltergeists are mean to her."

"She sounds a little sketchy. But now what?" Wendy asks.

"I have to figure out who stole the doll and killed Mr. Beasley. People in town are looking at me suspiciously. Word is getting around that I'm a person of interest."

"Did the sheriff mention if he has any leads?" Wendy presses.

"I assume he came to my house this morning because he doesn't."

"So, where do we start?" Juliet asks.

"I just found this in the parking lot." I tell them pulling the shoe from my pocket.

"Awww, it's a tiny shoe!" Wendy squeals.

"Yikes! Pretty sure you just summoned several neighborhood dogs with that!" Juliet responds, stuffing her fingers in her ears. "Did it come from the missing doll?" she asks.

"I don't know. It could have come from any doll, I guess. Maybe even a museum visitor. But I kept it just in case."

"What if the doll is possessed by a poltergeist, and she dropped her shoe as she ran off?" Wendy suggests with a gasp. "Like a creepy fairy tale!"

"That's not funny!" Juliet says, shuddering.

"Oh, come on, you don't really believe a doll could be possessed, do you?" Wendy asks.

"She lives with a talking ghost cat!" Juliet points to me. "Can we really doubt *anything* anymore?"

"If it belongs to the stolen doll, I bet the thief dropped it, but thanks for putting that Chuckie flashback in my head," I tell her.

"Oh, I saw that movie. It scared me to death." Juliet giggles. Her expression says she wants to watch it again, though.

"Can I see the shoe?" Wendy asks with her hand out.

"Sure!" I shrug, giving it to her.

She turns it over in her hand, scrutinizing it.

"Anything?" Juliet asks.

"No, but you're better at this sort of thing," she insists, handing it to her.

When Juliet takes it, her face clouds over.

"Better at what sort of thing?" I ask. "What's wrong?"

"Witches can often sense emotional energy stored in an object," Wendy says as if that explains everything. "Juliet is better at it than I am."

"All objects have energy," Juliet explains.

"Yes, I remember that from the physics class, I barely passed. But what is emotional energy?" I ask, still puzzled about what they're doing with the shoe.

"Objects store energy - both negative and positive. That beloved teddy bear your grandma gave you when you were three is threadbare and falling apart, but you can't bring your-self to get rid of it. Yet you don't know why..."

I nod, thinking of the ballerina necklace my mom gave me for my eighth birthday.

"It contains positive energy," Juliet says. "However, I sense dark energy in this shoe."

"Are you telling me the doll really is possessed? Assuming this shoe belongs to it?" I ask, not sure if I should be afraid or laugh.

"It's possible. Or it could just be a dark incident *surrounding* the object." Wendy explains. "Remember, we still don't know who the shoe belongs to."

"If I have to pick one of those, I pick door number two," I respond, staring at the shoe, horrified that I've been carrying it in my pocket.

When Juliet tries to give it back to me, I gasp and jump backward. I don't appreciate it when she and Wendy laugh.

"The shoe won't bite, silly." Wendy shakes her head.

"How do you know?" I retort.

"It isn't doing anything right now, is it?" Juliet points out.

"I don't know! What if it isn't doing anything to you because you're a witch?" Juliet and Wendy look at each other like they don't quite know how to respond to my sudden nervousness. "I wasn't raised in a magical community, if you recall. I still don't know how most of this works."

"Okay, fair enough, I promise you the shoe isn't possessed," Juliet insists.

"But what if the doll is?" I press.

"The shoe still isn't," Wendy sighs with exasperation.

"What if the doll is possessed, and she comes looking for her shoe? Then what?"

I can tell Juliet and Wendy are trying not to laugh again. But I assume I can trust them. At least somewhat.

"You promise to take it right back if something happens?"

"I swear," Juliet assures me.

"You guys promise not to shout *boo* when I touch it?" I insist.

"I might throw it at you instead!" Juliet tells me, clearly losing patience.

"All right, all right, give me the shoe."

When Juliet hands me the shoe, I can tell it's taking every ounce of Wendy's self-control not to shout boo. I admit it's probably something I would do.

I take the shoe back, and thankfully, it doesn't feel like anything. Same as before. I gingerly place it back in my pocket, using only two fingers. Like two fingers will somehow keep me safe.

"It would help if I knew more about poltergeists and their capabilities," I explain.

"Are the books I got you helping?" Wendy asks.

"Don't get me wrong; they're great research. I just wish there was someone to discuss these things with. Someone who could hash everything out with me. Not that you two aren't great at this but talking to a poltergeist expert would help even more. I know I have *ghost* experience, but not so much with poltergeists."

Wendy and Juliet stare at each other wide-eyed.

"What? Why are you looking at each other like that?" I quiz them.

"We may know someone," Wendy says.

"Who?"

"His name is Pavel Grace," Juliet tells me.

"Does he live in town?" I ask.

"He lives at the top of Red Mountain," Wendy says.

"Seriously? Someone lives up there?" I ask in surprise.

"Have you ever noticed when you're in the pool swimming laps, there's a giant tent at the top?" Juliet says.

"Yes! I keep meaning to ask if you know anything about it."

"That's where Pavel lives," Wendy says simply.

"Why does he live there?" I ask. I bet she's making this up.

"He's this eccentric hermit who likes to live off the grid."

"But does he know about poltergeists? Just because he's odd doesn't mean he knows about the paranormal," I point out.

"If anyone would know, it would be him." Wendy and Juliet nod at each other.

"How do I know I can trust him? Is he a wizard? A psychic? A medium? You haven't given me much to go on so far," I protest.

"No one really knows what he is because he won't say. We're not sure that even he knows for certain," Wendy explains.

"We've often thought he could be a mystic," Juliet explains. "They're much harder to define because their gifts are so unusual. It's like they're a combination of everything you just mentioned."

Wendy nods in agreement.

"So, how do you know he can help me?" I'm increasingly skeptical about this so-called guru. I need real answers, and I need them now.

"Whatever he is, we know for certain that he's a renowned paranormal scholar who has dedicated his life to studying paranormal incidents, especially in Colorado. You'll have to trust us on this one. If he doesn't have answers, no one will," Wendy tells me.

"Okay, so how can I reach him? Do I just call him? Does he text?" I ask.

Wendy and Juliet glance at each other again.

"What? What aren't you telling me?"

"You have to go to the top of the mountain," Juliet says reluctantly.

"Is there a ski lift that would take me up there?" I ask hopefully, knowing full well it's never that easy.

"It's funny you should mention it because there was at one point," Juliet tells me.

"Not anymore, though?" I ask.

"Not since the 1950s," Juliet says.

"So, how do I get up there? Does someone have a helicopter I don't know about?" I'm getting impatient here.

"You drive part way up the mountain on a winding dirt road and then hike the rest," Wendy explains.

"Oh dear, you know I'm not a mountain climber!" I protest.

"Don't worry, there aren't any steep rocks to scale, but the dirt path can be a bit tricky." Wendy warns me.

"Okay, well, I'm not sure I have a choice at this point."

"Oh, and there's one other thing," Juliet says, holding up a finger.

"Are you kidding me? Why do you guys do this to me? Do I have to sacrifice a goat? Promise him my firstborn? That's where I draw the line!"

"He requires an offering, but I swear no goats involved." Juliet holds up three fingers like that makes it more believable. This whole thing makes me increasingly nervous.

Wendy gets a piece of paper, and a pen from behind the bakery counter, scribbles something, then thrusts it at me.

I read it, throwing my hands in the air. "Okay, now I know you're joking. This is serious, you two!"

When I see their faces, I realize they *are* serious. "Fine. I'll bring the offering. But I swear if you're pulling my leg, I'll never speak to you again."

"Neither of us shouted boo when we handed you the shoe, right?" Wendy reminds me.

"I guess."

"When are you going to realize you can trust us?" Juliet asks.

"I do trust you. I just take small steps to do it."

Wendy hugs me as usual while Juliet gives me a reassuring smile. I promise to let them know what I learn from Pavel as I head out the door, in search of the offering.

10

I admit it. I'm white knuckling the drive up the steep, winding mountain road just a little bit. I know I don't want to make this journey after dark. Truthfully, I worry I shouldn't be doing this at all, but I'm desperate.

I realize I've gone as far as I can by car when I arrive at a clearing with space to park and a sign that reads, "No motorized vehicles beyond this point." The worn, wooden sign has a pair of feet carved in it to emphasize its point.

I unload everything I might need from the back seat of the bus. Backpack with the special offering? Check. Water? Check. Hat? Check. Proper hiking boots? Check. Confidence? Nope! I left that back in town.

I'm nervous about meeting this so-called mystic who lives atop a mountain. Who would want to live up here? What if this is a colossal waste of time? *No*, I scold myself. You can trust Wendy and Juliet. This has to be the right thing.

It takes an hour to reach the top of the mountain and the tent. It's clear that a forest fire tore through here once. Some trees are growing back, but others are still just burnt skeletons of their former selves.

The elevation is nearly 8,000 feet above sea level. Despite my dedicated weekly cardio workouts, I'm practically gasping for breath when I arrive at Pavel's doorstep. If tents have doorsteps, that is.

"Hello!" I call out. What if he isn't home? It's not like I could have called to tell him I'm coming. Juliet and Wendy insisted he'd just know.

My imagination ran wild during my hike. I formed a detailed picture of what a mountain top mystic looks like. I just know he has a shaved head, wears a simple burlap robe he stitched by hand, and spends his days sitting criss-cross apple sauce while meditating for hours at a time.

I'm also convinced he'll speak in riddles, serve me a special homegrown tea, like Wendy's brews, then, out of the blue, the answer to one of his riddles will hit me. My life will change forever.

Instead, I nearly gasp out loud upon seeing this sage for the first time. I know it's rude, but I can't help myself. The bald man in a scratchy robe turns out to be a throwback from a bygone era. I think he looks far more suited to drive my VW bus than me.

Rather than a shaved head, he wears his hair long in the back, pulled into a ponytail. On top of his head are a handful of wispy hairs I could probably count by hand if I wanted to. Small round glasses with pink lenses perch on the end of his nose.

"Yo, man!" he exclaims. He doesn't seem surprised to find an unannounced stranger in his presence.

"Um, yo?" I respond.

"Did you bring the offering?" he asks eagerly.

"Yes!" I tell him, gently placing my backpack on the floor then removing the offering as if it were the most precious artifact in the world. I carefully hand the bag of pork rinds to him. Yes, I said pork rinds. You thought it must be something else? Me too.

"Groovy! Thanks, dude!" he exclaims eagerly, tearing the bag open. "Want some?" he asks, holding the bag out to me.

"Uh, no, thanks, I'm trying to cut back." I've never had a pork rind in my life, and I don't intend to start now. I'm more of a Cheeze-Its kind of gal. Cheeze-Its dipped in peanut butter. Don't knock it until you've tried it!

"I don't mean to be rude. I would have called first to let you know I was coming, but..." I let myself trail off. This whole thing seems absurd. Once again, I remind myself that Juliet and Wendy have never given me a reason not to trust them, and they wouldn't send me this far on a prank, but I feel like it's seriously pushing the boundaries here.

"Don't worry, dove, I knew you were coming," he smiles at me. "Thanks for the pork rinds!"

"Well, uh, I'm told that you're the person to ask about--"

"Poltergeists!"

"Yes. How did you... Never mind." I shrug.

"Have a seat. Make yourself at home." He points to a colorful rug on the ground. We sit across from each other, criss-cross apple sauce. I got that part right, at least.

"I don't know how much you already know, so I'll just start with the basics if that's all right with you," he tells me.

I nod my head excitedly. I hope he can teach me as much as Wendy and Juliet say he can.

"Poltergeists are a tricky lot. Never trust one, by the way. They're master manipulators. Also, they aren't confined to one place like your traditional spirits, as I'm guessing you already know as a spirit communicator. They can attach themselves to a person or a place or possibly even an object. I assume you're asking because you think a poltergeist killed Mr. Beasley?"

This time I nod reluctantly. I don't even question how he automatically knows all these things. I'm not sure I would understand it, anyway. I cringe before asking the following question because I can't believe I'm even doing it. "This may sound extra weird, but I have to ask."

Pavel laughs. "You want to ask me if I think a poltergeist has inhabited the missing doll? You're secretly worried a possessed doll is now running throughout Glenwood Springs terrorizing residents and chasing cats up trees?"

I blush and stammer. "I didn't quite picture the doll sneaking through town and terrorizing people, but..." I trail off. Okay, I kind of did.

He nods his head. I appreciate him not treating me like he thinks I'm a lunatic. "It could certainly happen. But it's unlikely. Even if it did, the doll would have physical limitations."

"Like?"

"Like a two-foot-tall doll, for example, no matter how powerful the poltergeist who possessed it was, couldn't drive a car."

"But could it push over a solid oak bookcase?" I still can't believe I'm asking these questions. But as long as I have a mystic expert on the paranormal sitting in front of me eating pork rinds, I know I must.

"Crushed by a heavy bookcase," he shudders. "What a gruesome ending."

"For certain. But could a doll possessed by a poltergeist push it over?"

"Given the proper momentum, I would say yes, man."

"What about just your basic poltergeist?" I continue.

"Definitely." He nods.

"You also mentioned they can attach themselves to a person? How does that work? Do they possess that person?"

"As in 'the poltergeist made me do it?'" He smiles.

"Yeah, kind of," I sheepishly admit.

"When a poltergeist attaches themselves to a person, it's more like an obsession than a haunting, if that's what you're thinking," he patiently explains.

"I don't follow you."

"Why did Mr. Beasley hire you in the first place?" he asks.

"He hoped I could reason with the poltergeists who haunt the museum. He told me they'd been there for as long as he could remember. They played tricks and engaged in the usual poltergeist hijinks."

"So why now? Why hire you to *reason* with them, as you say?"

"He explained that recently they were acting increasingly hostile and obnoxious," I tell him.

"So, what changed?" he presses.

"Nothing that I know of," I answer.

Pavel shakes his head. "Something must have changed. The energy under which the poltergeists exist was altered. They wouldn't change their behavior that drastically for no reason."

I pause, trying to remember if Mr. Beasley had indicated any drastic changes. "He was bringing in a rare and extremely valuable doll from a collection in Denver?" I say it like a question because it's all I can think of.

"The possessed doll that's terrorizing the town?" he asks, an impish gleam in his eye.

I shrug. "Like I said, it's all I've got."

"That can't be it. It would have to be something far more significant. A large shift in the museum's energy pattern."

"I'm sorry, I just don't know," I tell him.

"If you can determine that--"

"I'll find the killer?" I interrupt hopefully.

"I didn't say that. But it would explain the poltergeists' behavior shift," he says.

I must appear as crestfallen as I feel because he quickly adds, "You never know, it *could* lead to the killer! Does he have an angry ex-wife, by chance?"

"Not that I know of." I think the sheriff might have mentioned that.

"But getting back to your original question about what happens when a poltergeist becomes obsessed with a person."

"Yes!" I exclaim. There's so much to take in here. I don't know how I'll remember it all.

"A poltergeist who's attached to a person will stalk them, play tricks on them, mess with their minds, those sorts of things."

"Could they kill them?" I ask, half afraid of the answer.

"Oh, my, yes. If they're angry enough and their obsession becomes uncontrollable. By the way, don't assume you can *reason* with a poltergeist without offering them something. You have to give them a very good reason," he insists.

"Incentives matter?" I ask.

"Exactly!" he exclaims excitedly.

"How about this," I suggest. "What happens if I got rid of all the negative energy they're feeding off?"

"Oh, my child, all the pot in the world couldn't erase that much negative energy. The museum poltergeists aren't your only suspects, are they?" he asks.

"At this point, they kind of are. The Sheriff's Department thinks I'm a person of interest because they found me trying to lift the bookcase off Mr. Beasley. I don't know of anyone else."

"Do you know Remy Cashmore?" he asks.

"No."

"Ms. Cashmore is an eccentric doll collector who, I would argue, has always been Mr. Beasley's rival. She used to work at the doll museum until they had a falling out, and he fired her."

"You think *she* could have killed Mr. Beasley?" I ask hopefully.

"Possibly. If you're going to investigate this case to clear your name, you should talk to her," he suggests.

The questions pour out of me. I had no mentors growing up. There was no one I could discuss these kinds of things with, and it's not like I was going to check out a book in the middle school library - Poltergeists 101.

Even researching this as an adult meant admitting what I was capable of, so forget that. I know so little about so much of this. It's a relief to be open with someone.

"I have to ask, why here? Why live on the top of a mountain by yourself?" I expect him to tell me he's down on his luck, maybe even homeless. Perhaps society refused to accept him as a mystic, so they banished him to this mountaintop. If that's the case, I'll be really mad. He's obviously harmless. How could society shun him like this? The more I think about it, the madder I get.

"I got rich," he says.

"You got rich?" I did *not* expect him to say that. Why would a person get rich and then live like this? I think he's teasing me.

"I correctly predicted that Colorado would legalize pot, so I founded the biggest pot store chain in the state."

My mouth falls open, but no words come out.

"I'm sure you've seen The Groovy Greens Pot Stores?" he asks.

"Oh yeah, they're in Glenwood. I've seen them in Denver too."

"Those are mine."

"No way!" I exclaim in shock.

"Is that *groovy* or what?" He grins.

"I still don't get why you live on the top of the mountain in a tent."

"You mean instead of a mansion in Aspen where I hobnob with the movie stars?" he asks.

"Yeah, kind of."

"That just isn't my scene man. I've always dreamed of living in the middle of nowhere." He spreads his arms wide.

"Don't you get lonely?" I ask.

"Sometimes. But on the rare occasion that I do, I go into town, swim in the hot springs, visit a brewery, check on my stores, all good stuff. What I don't miss are noisy, annoying neighbors that make me want to pull out what little hair I have left."

I nod. It makes sense in a weird way. It must be so peaceful up here.

Pavel rubs his hands together. "Now, let's talk about you, dove. I've never met a spirit communicator. You obviously know how rare you are."

"Yes."

"Would you like to know a secret?" he giggles.

"Sure?"

"I'm so jazzed about meeting you, I'm about to burst." He pumps his fist in the air.

"Me?" I ask. This guy is so complex.

"You're one of the few remaining boxes on my paranormal bingo card. I don't know if your friends told you, but I've studied the paranormal my entire life and experienced a lot of far-out stuff. You're the first spirit communicator, though."

"Do I win a prize?" I ask half jokingly, but you never know.

Pavel laughs uproariously. "You're funny too!" he shouts, stuffing another pork rind in his mouth, chewing noisily.

I'm still not sure how to take this man. Are all mystics like this? I can see why he prefers to live on a mountain top.

"I was particularly impressed with how you saved the spirits at the Red Castle Hotel," he tells me.

"How did you know that, too? Oh, wait, did you just *know* that?" I ask.

"No, I read about it in the newspaper! An owl brings me a copy of the Gazette every day." When my jaw drops once again, he guffaws. "I'm joking! But you should see your face."

"I recently moved into a house with a talking ghost cat, so I'll believe almost anything these days," I explain.

"Now *that* is outta sight!" he thunders. "A talking ghost cat! That can't be real."

"Oh, that's real." I laugh back. Some days I can barely believe it myself.

"Get out. Does this talking ghost cat have a name?" he asks eagerly.

"Mystery."

"It's a mystery, or the name is Mystery?" he presses.

"Her name is Mystery," I tell him.

He slaps his hand on his knee. "Holly, you are a fascinating person! Tell me more. Did this cat talk before she was deceased?"

"I'm not sure. I never thought to ask her," I admit.

"You must ask her! Then report back to me next time you see me."

"That's a deal," I tell him. "Now, as fascinating and helpful as this has been, and I truly appreciate your time, I must get home. I don't want to travel the mountain in the dark."

I hate having to leave him. I would love to learn more about being a mystic, but if I stay around any longer, I'll regret it. I can't hike in the dark.

Pavel jumps up. "I completely understand, and I'm thrilled you stopped by. Until we meet again!" He bows at me. I'm not sure what to do with that, so I just stick out my hand to shake his. He's truly one of the most fascinating people I've ever met.

"One more thing Holly," he stops me as I step out of the tent.

"Yes?"

"Remember, there's strength in numbers. You've made some wonderful new friends in town. You don't have to do everything yourself," he tells me.

I nod. Is there anything he doesn't know? I sure wish he knew who killed Mr. Beasley!

11

We talked far longer than I anticipated, so there's very little daylight left. The shadows grow longer and longer as I walk. The evening air is chilly up here.

Just as I reach the bus it's dark out. I hate the idea of driving down the narrow dirt road like this, but what other choice do I have? I'd rather drive down a dirt road in the dark than sleep in a tent, that's for sure. If I drive slowly and carefully, I'll be fine.

It could be good practice for when I have to travel in the snow this winter. Not something I ever had to do in Florida, so I'm already nervous about it. I've seen pictures of Glenwood Canyon in a snowstorm. It's breathtakingly beautiful, but I don't want to drive in it.

I wish Clara and Mystery were here to keep me company. Clara would think it was exciting. Mystery would bark out, well, meow instructions from the back seat.

The night is black as ink. When I gaze up into the sky, I gasp. I never realized there were that many stars. That must be the Milky Way, which I didn't know a person could actually see from the ground. I always assumed I'd need a telescope.

But when you're in the middle of a mountain, away from the lights in town, apparently you can see everything. When I see a shooting star, I gasp again. How did I not know about this?

But as unbelievable as the stars are, I still have to get down this treacherous mountain. I grip the steering wheel so hard my knuckles are white. If I thought it was scary earlier, that was nothing. I don't plan to do it again anytime soon.

Then I remember someone once said that you only have to see as far as your headlights. Who the heck was that? It was in a movie, I think. Just keep following the headlights, and eventually, you'll get home. Remembering that makes me feel better. I've so got this handled. Only about 20 minutes more to go. Not a problem. I even relax a tiny bit.

Then the VW stops. Just comes to a sputtering halt in the middle of a pitch-black mountain road. Fiddlesticks!

12

"No! No! No!" I pound on the steering wheel. I just got this car, and it's quitting on me already? Out here? In the middle of nowhere?

Tom, my mechanic, said it was in great shape. I can't believe I'm stuck on a mountain in the dark. I jump when a coyote howls. What's scratching against the side of the bus?

Every teen angst horror movie I've ever seen flashes through my head. The only thing missing is a teenage boy trying to convince teenage me to make out with him.

Of all the ways I may have pictured dying, this certainly wasn't one of them. I see brief flashes and swirls of light among the trees. It must be ghosts. Or maybe it's my imagination. If they're ghosts, it means they died here. I don't want to think about that.

I wonder how long it would take to walk home? It might take all of five minutes if I get eaten by a coyote or a bear or bit by a poisonous snake. What kind of snakes do they have in the Colorado mountains? Never mind. I don't want to know.

My mind whirls like an out-of-control roller coaster. I pull out my phone to make a call. My hand shakes while nervous sweat drips down my back. AAA comes out here, right? Argh! Of course, there's no signal.

Nationwide coverage, my foot, I grumble. They should include an asterisk. Nationwide coverage except on the side of a dark mountain where you're certain to be murdered by a madman with a hook for a hand. Now I'm having a panic attack. I seriously feel like I can't breathe. What to do? What to do?

When I'm blinded by ultra-bright lights, I really freak out. Am I hallucinating? Have I already died, and this is the light I'm supposed to go into? I didn't picture it like this. Should I stay and be a ghost? Clara, Mystery, and I could drive around in the pink bus and do stuff.

We'll need someone to drive of course. I'll have to track down another spirit communicator to do that. Which could take forever. What if I'm *not* dead yet, but this is the killer?

You know, the killer from the slasher movies? It's weird what goes through a person's head when they're about to die. Now the lights are flashing blue and red. Do killers have police lights?

They're still so bright I can't see clearly. I think I need a paper bag to breathe into. I hold my hand in front of my eyes like I'm squinting into the sunlight. When I see a large man approaching my car, I scream. I don't even have a decent weapon. Where's a good hammer when I need one?

"Holly!" the large man with a hook for a hand shouts.

The hook man knows my name.

Wait, it's not a slasher, it's Sheriff Mack! What is he doing here? I jump out of the bus.

"Sheriff! How did you know I was here?" I exclaim in shock.

"Once again, your friends came to your rescue," he shouts back.

"Wendy and Juliet sent you?" I gasp, struggling to slow down my breathing. My heart continues to race uncomfortably.

"They called the station to report you missing. Said you hadn't checked in since you headed off to Red Mountain," he tells me.

"I was driving down the mountain, and my bus just died. I don't know what happened."

"Hang on a sec. I'll check it out." He retrieves a handheld flood light from his SUV then saunters to the back of the bus. He opens the hatch and pokes around for a bit. "Here it is. You're missing a bolt in the alternator."

I stare at him unblinkingly. The voices in my head tell me not to say it, but I can't help it.

"Are you telling me I have a screw loose?"

He stares back at me. Perhaps side-of-the-dark-mountain-humor wasn't called for here.

"Do you have a pen?" he sighs.

"Yeah, let me get it." I dig around in the glove box, finally locating a pen. "Will this work?" I ask?

He takes it from me and does something with it inside the engine. I don't know how he expects to fix a dead bus with a pen, but I'll trust he knows what he's doing.

"Try it now," he grunts.

Still skeptical, I step up into the driver's seat, and turn the key. Well color me shocked. The bus fires to life. Sheriff Mack closes the hatch then walks up to the driver's side window.

"Follow me out of here, and you'll be fine to get home. Then check with Tom tomorrow about replacing the pen with the proper bolt."

"How did this happen? Tom just changed the oil and checked everything over to make sure it was okay. How did a bolt just fall out?"

"It's bumpy terrain along here. May have worked its way loose," he explains.

"Thank you. Truly. I appreciate it." I tell him. I mean it.

"Just doing my job." He tips his hat at me, then strolls back to his car.

He makes a u-turn turns on the narrow path, slowly driving back down the dirt road so I don't lose track of him. When we finally get to the bottom of the mountain, he flashes his lights then drives back toward the station while I drive home with my hands still shaking from the unwanted excitement.

13

Clara is waiting for me on the patio, upset once again. "Where have you been?" she cries. "I've been worried sick."

"I had car trouble."

"It seems to be okay now," she points out.

"Sheriff Mack fixed it. At least temporarily."

"Awww, I bet he did!" she coos.

I roll my eyes at her obvious crush, even though I'm feeling incredibly grateful for his repeated help. It's a complicated relationship. "Let me text Wendy and Juliet and tell them I'm home. Then I'll fill you in on everything."

I thank the ladies for sending help, assuring them I'll update everyone later. Then I collapse into the nearest comfortable chair to relay the story to my roommates. I'm exhausted, but if I don't do it now, I won't get a moment's peace from them. I repeat my conversation with Pavel, including the part about Remy.

"Do either of you know a Remy Cashmore? Pavel said she was a rival doll collector?"

"Yes!" Clara exclaims. "She lives in the Mountain Peaks Mobile Home Park on the west side of town."

"Any chance you know her exact address?"

"Oh, you'll know it when you see it," Mystery laughs.

"What's that supposed to mean?" I ask.

"Just wait," Clara says while she and Mystery nod knowingly at each other.

Why does it seem like everyone else in this town, including a cat, knows more than I do about these things?

"Fine. Pavel said if I'm investigating this case, I should interview her as a suspect. I assume you want to come with me?"

"Yes, please!" Clara pumps her fist.

"I also have to stop at Tom's place again tomorrow to get a bolt for the bus, but I think it will be okay to see Remy first."

The following morning, I coast slowly through the Mountain Peaks Mobile Home Park, wondering how I'll ever know which one is Remy's house. It's a small park with a handful of streets. The homes are cozy but tidy. Most have yards with fences. Several have flower gardens and decorations in the front.

Then I see it. The house with dolls. Everywhere. Dolls of every shape, size, and color on display. Dolls on chairs, dolls in hammocks, dolls posing with garden gnomes. There's even a doll pretending to mow the lawn with a miniature lawn mower.

"Told you," Clara murmurs.

"We must be here," I respond.

"This is still the freakiest thing I've ever seen," Mystery says, her paws balanced on the windowsill, her face pressed so close to the window, there's a circle of steam. Her tail swishes in amazement.

I park in front of Remy's house, pausing to gawk at the display. I wonder if her neighbors mind the collection. I guess they don't have a choice. I remind myself that I'm here to do a job, forcing myself to leave the VW while still staring at the scene.

I slowly push open the gate, careful not to step on any of the displays, but as I approach the house, a doll waves at me in greeting, startling me so badly I jump straight in the air. It must be on a motion sensor, but it scared the heck out of me.

When I hear Clara and Mystery laughing I whip around to glare at them. I ring Remy's doorbell, and the song Hello Dolly plays in the background. Of course.

When Remy answers the door, I'm stunned. I thought Pavel was an interesting-looking person, but Remy certainly wins that prize. I have to look down at her because she's about as short as she is wide. I don't think she's even five feet tall.

I'm unsure if her curly black hair is natural or a wig. She blinks up at me through thick round glasses that magnify her already enormous eyes, yet none of these compare to her eyebrows. I swear it appears as if she drew on her eyebrows with a thick, black, felt tip marker. I try desperately not to stare. From the doorway, I can see a living room stuffed full of dolls.

"Can I help you?" she asks.

"Er, yes," I mumble, trying to remember why I'm here. There's just so much to see. I feel like I've entered an alternate reality.

"Hello?" she tries again.

"Oh, hi, sorry about that. I'm Holly Daniel, and I'm a Paranormal Private Investigator. I'm looking into the murder of Mr. Beasley and the doll theft from the museum. I was hoping I could ask you some questions?"

"Yes, of course. Come right in, dear," she says opening the screen door with a sweeping gesture to welcome me into her home. "Have a seat. Would you like some tea?"

"Oh, uh, sure." I'm so entranced by all the dolls I barely hear her talking.

I mistakenly assume I can move a doll to sit down because there is no empty chair, but as I reach for one, Remy shouts.

"Not there!"

I recoil like a scolded child whose hand got smacked while reaching for a hot stove.

"That's Tammy's seat. She says you can't sit there."

"Oh! Is there a better spot?" I ask.

Remy then talks to the dolls, asking which one would like me to sit with them.

"Bella, could the nice lady who has come to visit, sit with you?"

For a moment, I'm amused she talks to the dolls as if they can hear her. But then I recall how kids made fun of me for talking to what they assumed were imaginary friends.

I shouldn't judge. Perhaps these dolls really are her friends. Plus, she's being so nice to me when she could have slammed the door in my face and yelled at me to get off her lawn.

"Bella says you can sit with her," Remy tells me, pointing to the blue chair in the corner.

I reach for Bella.

"Gently please!" Remy scolds.

I gingerly pick up Bella with two hands, holding her up.

"Where would you like me to put her?"

"What do you mean?" Remy asks.

"Where do I put her so I can sit down?" What does she mean, what do I mean?

"She'll sit on your lap, of course. It's her chair. She's just allowing you to share it."

"Of course." I never imagined this scenario when I signed up to be a private investigator. I sit in Bella's chair, carefully holding her in my lap.

"She likes you," Remy tells me.

"She's very nice," I respond, because I can't think of anything else to say.

While Remy prepares our tea, I take a moment to stare at her layout. I half hope that the stolen doll is sitting on a shelf in this room, so I can call Sheriff Mack to come out to arrest her. She seems very nice so far, but I want my name cleared.

Then it occurs to me I'm casually sitting in the home of a person I think could have killed Mr. Beasley and stolen a $20,000 doll, yet I don't have backup. Nor does anyone know I'm here. Why do I keep doing this?

I continue to twist my head as I drink in the sights. Every square inch of Remy's home has something doll related. Some dolls are featured in display cases, while others, like the ones outside, are posed in various activities. There's a small red table in the corner with three dolls, wearing formal costumes, having their own version of a tea party.

Then there's a little wooden school desk with a doll wearing a student uniform. There are cheerleader dolls, football player dolls, and animal dolls. I can't begin to count them. If Remy stole the rare doll, I might not even notice. It could be sitting here at this moment, and I can't see it.

Although I have to assume a $20,000 rare, autographed collectible would be on special display. Of course, if she stole it after murdering Mr. Beasley, I don't think she'd show it in her living room.

What if she hid in another room! I plot ways to get into those rooms while she hums a song and continues to prepare the tea. Perhaps after a while I could tell her I need to use the bathroom.

Remy returns with a matching, but human-sized version of the tea set the dolls in the corner are using. She places an intricate doily on the table next to me along with a teacup, which she then fills with tea. Then she hands me a miniature teacup as well, telling me, "This is for Bella." Of course, it is.

I take the cup from her. "Hold it steady," she insists. While I do that, she gets the miniature teapot from the table in the corner, pretending to pour tea into the tiny cup. I still can't believe this is happening. "Go ahead, help her drink it!" she urges. I hold the teacup up to Bella's mouth and pretend to tip the air tea into it.

"She says thank you," Remy smiles.

"That's nice," I smile back, placing the empty miniature teacup on the end table while picking up my own to take a sip. Remy sits opposite me with two dolls on her lap.

"Do you have your own children, Holly?" she asks.

"No," I respond, wondering why she's asking me that.

"Are you married?" she presses.

It always makes me uncomfortable when the subject comes up. I don't enjoy getting into my personal life with people I know. I *really* don't enjoy getting into it with strangers.

"I'm a widow."

"Oh dear, at such a young age. Even so, plenty of time to have children, and you'll love it when you do. I promise," she says, gesturing to the dolls.

"No doubt," I respond, nodding my head.

"Awful news about Mr. Beasley," she shakes her head sorrowfully. "Who could have done such a thing?"

"That's what I'm hoping to find out," I tell her. I continue to scan each doll's face, hoping to find a clue. This is worse than the museum. I feel like these dolls are watching us.

"What is your interest in Mr. Beasley? Do you collect dolls too? You said you're an investigator?" Remy asks eagerly.

"I'm a Paranormal Private Investigator. Mr. Beasley hired me to deal with some misbehaving poltergeists that were causing him trouble in the doll museum. He was worried about the rare doll that was arriving from Denver and didn't want any trouble."

"But now that he's dead, you're investigating his murder?" she asks.

"Yes. The doll theft as well," I explain.

"Did you see the special doll when she arrived at the museum?" Remy presses. "I think she's a work of art."

I shake my head. "I was there before the doll arrived."

"Oh, that's too bad," she says.

"Do you mind if I ask where you were when Mr. Beasley was killed?"

"Why are you curious about that? Do you think *I* killed him? Did the cops say something to you?" she asks, suddenly agitated by my query.

"No, of course not. Haven't you heard? I'm a person of interest in the murder."

"I thought you said you arrived after he was killed!" she exclaims.

"Yes, but when Sheriff Mack showed up, I was trying to lift the bookcase off Mr. Beasley but couldn't. The cops thought I pushed it on him."

"The bookcase is very heavy. I don't think you could pick it up on your own." She shakes her head.

I don't ask her how she would know that because I don't want to make her suspicious of my motives. Pavel said she used to work there, so perhaps that's how she knows, but she looks guiltier by the moment to me.

"I wish I could be of more use," she continues. "Do you know if the sheriff found anything interesting?"

"What do you mean, interesting?"

"You know, on tv, they always find some interesting clue that the bad guy accidentally left behind," she explains.

"Even if they did, I doubt they'd tell me. Considering I'm a person of interest."

"Yes, good point. I suppose you're right," she says thoughtfully.

"I don't mean to be pushy, but where were you again?" I ask.

"Oh! Yes, of course. I was in Colorado Springs picking up my most recent acquisition," she points to a doll on the shelf.

"What is her name?" I ask.

"Lily," she tells me proudly.

I place Bella back in the chair and move closer to see Lily. Lily has big green eyes, and her coloring is a tawny beige, but what's most unique about her is the tiny lily painted on her cheek.

"She's beautiful. So delicate." I murmur.

"Yes, she is. She's a one of a kind, there's no other like her in the world," Remy proudly tells me.

"Hey, could I use your bathroom?" I ask.

"Of course, dear, just go through that door, to your left, then the first door on the right."

"I'll just be a moment!" I assure her. Someone like Remy would have an expensive doll on display somewhere in the house. If I could just peek into the other rooms, I might catch a glimpse. Not surprisingly, the bathroom is just as full of doll-themed decorations as the rest of the house.

I notice the doll-themed shower curtain in addition to a grinning doll's face looking up at me from the toilet lid. I think I could have done without that one.

I finish in the bathroom, wash my hands, and then dry them with a towel held by a doll. Slowly, I crack open the door. I'm worried that Remy might be waiting right outside for me, but the coast is clear.

I tiptoe down the hallway toward the room at the end. This room is also full of dolls. She has enough dolls in this house to start her own museum. I glance behind me to make sure she still hasn't come looking for me as I venture into the room.

I search quickly, hoping to spot the collectible before it's too late. Dolls, dolls, and more dolls. Remy could hide it in plain sight, and if I didn't know exactly what I was looking for, it would be hard to spot in here. Then I see a large lockbox on the floor next to what looks like a brand new, yet empty, display case.

My heart hammers inside my chest so loud I'm convinced Remy will hear it from the living room. This has to be it. A display case waiting for a special doll. I glance behind me once again. In every mystery novel I've ever read, the victim always gets obsessed with looking at whatever, and the bad guy sneaks up on them from behind.

I can't let Remy do that. I obviously don't have formal investigative training, but I like to think one can learn a lot from the novels. At the very least, they've taught me what not to do.

"Everything okay in there, dear?" Remy calls out from the living room.

"I'll be right there!" I call back. I hope that didn't sound too weird?

That lockbox has to have the doll in it. I just know it. I ponder if I should just text Sheriff Mack right here and now or try to open the lockbox on my own first. But then what?

I see the doll and run? Or confront Remy? She's already killed once over it. She could do it again. I must know what's in the box. Could it be unlocked? It's now or never I murmur, reaching for the handle.

"**W**ould you like some more tea?"

I scream. How embarrassing. I just swore I wouldn't get caught unaware, yet here I am.

Then Remy screams because I startled her too, I guess.

"What are you doing in here?" she demands. "Why did you scream?"

"Why did *you* scream?" I ask.

"You scared me."

"Well, you scared me too!" I exclaim, planting my hands onto my hips.

"I thought you had to go to the bathroom," she reminds me.

"I did. Then I noticed this room on my way out, and I wanted to see more of your beautiful dolls!"

"Oh," she relaxes. "There are so many!"

"Yes, there are! I'm really curious about who goes in this display case."

"I haven't decided yet," she claims. "You know, actually, the dolls in this room are shy. That's why they aren't in the living room. Come now, I don't want to upset them. Why don't we go back into the other room?"

While we stroll back into the living room, I realize I won't get any more out of Remy today. "I really must be going now but thank you for your time and the tea. If you hear anything about the stolen doll, will you please let me know?" I ask, handing her my business card.

"Of course, dear," she says, staring up at me. I just know I'll have weird dreams now about dolls staring at me with painted-on eyebrows. Remy leads me out onto the patio, where we exchange more pleasantries, but then I see Clara waving frantically at me to return to the bus. I almost shout *what is it*, but I don't want to startle Remy further. Instead, I shoot Clara a steely eyed glare.

When I remember the shoe in my pocket, I nearly ask Remy about it. If anyone would know what kind of doll it belongs to, I'm sure it's her. Yet, for some reason, my instincts stop me. I think it's best I keep it to myself. For now, anyway.

"One more thing!" Remy grabs my arm before I can leave.

"If you're looking for suspects, check out Dustin Holmes. For years, his family has insisted that the Bebe Mothereau doll belongs to them."

"Really? Where can I find this Dustin Holmes?"

"His office is in the financial district. Holmes Conglomerated I think it's called. Their whole family is filthy rich so he should be easy to find."

"Thank you for everything!" I tell her, still careful to avoid disturbing the displays in her yard.

When I finally get back to the bus, I round on Clara. "What is wrong with you?" I hiss.

"When you were inside, I saw a man lurking outside Remy's house!" she exclaims.

"What did he look like?"

"It was hard to tell exactly. He wore a dark hoodie covering part of his face, so I couldn't see clearly," she tells me.

"But what did he *look* like? Tall, short, somewhere in between?" This is frustrating.

"He was quite tall."

"Anything else? Can you tell what color hair he had?" I continue to ask.

"No, just that he was sneaking around Remy's yard," she tells me.

"Do you think it was a neighbor?"

"Maybe. But even if it was a neighbor, he looked suspicious."

"I didn't see anybody," Mystery chimes in.

"So, how did you see someone," I point to Clara. "But you didn't," I point at Mystery. "Are you sure you saw someone sneaking around, or was it just someone walking by? Or maybe it was a lawn care man."

Clara glares at Mystery. "You didn't see him because you were sound asleep in the backseat!"

"Oh yeah, huh? I think it was nap number 11 for today." Mystery laughs.

I start up the bus and pull away from Remy's house. That was one of the strangest encounters I've ever had. I need to know what is in the lockbox, but how? I'm not sure what to think about Clara and the mysterious man either.

"Did you learn anything helpful? Did she admit to killing Mr. Beasley?" Clara asks as if it could be that easy.

"She claims she was in Colorado Springs getting a new doll for her collection when he was killed," I tell her.

"Do you believe her?"

"I don't know. Obviously, I'll check it out. Do you know her entire house is full of dolls?" I ask.

"I'm not surprised, given the state of her yard." Clara shakes her head.

"She also said something suspicious. When I told her the Sheriff's Department considers me a person of interest, she seemed surprised by that, then pointed out that I arrived after Mr. Beasley died."

"What's suspicious about that?" Clara asks. "It's true, isn't it?"

"*I* didn't tell her that."

"What *did* you say?" Clara asks.

"Nothing specific. Just that I was a person of interest. I didn't say why or when."

"Oh, that is odd," she responds thoughtfully.

"Very."

"Where to next?" Mystery asks.

"Next, we visit Tom to see if he can replace the missing bolt on the alternator."

"You sound so smart!" Clara tells me.

I shrug. "I'm just repeating what Sheriff Mack said. I don't know what any of that even means."

15

Tom comes out to greet us before I can slide the bus into park.

"Hey there, Holly," he calls out. "How's the bus running?"

"Not so great," I tell him.

"What do you mean? What's wrong with her?"

"She broke down on Red Mountain last night."

"Are you serious? What happened? She's running now, obviously."

"Sheriff Mack rescued me. He said a bolt fell off the alternator?" I scratch my head. "I don't even know what that means."

"Ah, let me guess. He replaced the missing bolt with a pen."

"That's exactly what he did!" I exclaim.

"Smart man, that sheriff." Tom smiles.

I almost laugh out loud when I spot Clara hanging out the window, nodding her head vigorously.

"Let's see what we can find, shall we?" he says, peering into the engine. "Yep, the bolt fell out. Where did you say you were?"

"Red Mountain."

"Hmmm, it's bumpy terrain there. It must have jiggled loose. I think I have a replacement for it. Should take about 30 minutes."

"Perfect," I tell him. "I'll wait at the bookstore."

When Tom disappears into the garage searching for a bolt, I wag my finger at Clara and Mystery. "Behave you guys. I'm going to Wendy's store."

"Hey there, W--"

"Holly! I'm so relieved!" Wendy launches herself at me, hugging me so hard she nearly knocks me down. "You're okay, right?"

"I'm fine. I swear."

"What happened? We were so worried when we didn't hear from you." She holds me out at arm's length, refusing to let go.

"Pavel and I talked forever, but on the way back, the bus died on me. That's why I'm here. Tom is fixing it right now."

"How can that be? Didn't you say he checked it over recently?" She's practically shrieking; she's still so upset.

"Some kind of bolt worked its way loose and fell out."

"You must have been so scared out there alone. Why didn't you call?" She smacks me on the arm.

"No cell service," I shrug. "Thank goodness you called Sheriff Mack."

"Hmm," she says.

"What?" I glare at her.

"How many times has he rescued you?"

"Whatever. I'm grateful you called him and that he went out there."

"What did Pavel tell you? Anything interesting?"

I relay everything I talked about with Pavel while Wendy takes it in wordlessly. I can rarely shock *her* into speechlessness.

"Oh, and then there's Remy Cashmore," I add.

"The doll collector! Why didn't I think of that? She and Mr. Beasley had a huge fight once, and he fired her. I bet she'd love to get her hands on that collectible doll!"

"That was my thought exactly after Pavel told me about her," I nod. "Plus, I think I saw it in her house."

"What? Did you tell Sheriff Mack yet?" Wendy exclaims.

"No, let me clarify. I think I saw the lockbox she's keeping it in."

"I'm not following," she says, squinting at me in confusion.

"I went to the bathroom. Then, when she wasn't looking, I snuck into another room."

Wendy gasps.

"That room had a lock box just the right size for the doll Mr. Beasley showed us, and it had an expensive display case. One you'd use for a rare doll."

"Let me get this straight. You went to someone's house who you think killed Mr. Beasley *and* stole the collector's doll, but you haven't told the sheriff yet."

"Uhhh, when you put it like that."

"Holly!" She smacks me on the arm again. "You shouldn't do these things alone!"

"It's too late for that now," I remind her. "Besides, she says she was in Colorado Springs picking up yet another collectible doll when Mr. Beasley was killed."

"How do you know she was telling the truth?"

"I saw it on a shelf in her living room. It has a lily painted on its cheek, and her name is Lily, of course. She says it was one of a kind."

Wendy gasps again.

"What now?" I ask.

She dives below the store countertop. Then I hear her rummaging among papers. She pops up with a stack of magazines a moment later.

"Hang on a sec," she mutters, leafing through the stack. "Here it is." She rapidly thumbs through the pages in search of what I desperately hope is something important.

I don't know how she remembers these things. Whenever I ask her a question if she's seen it in a book or a magazine or a newspaper, she remembers it. "Yep! Got it!" she mumbles again. She triumphantly brandishes a magazine called Mountain Life.

"What is that?" I ask. "I don't get it."

She opens it to show me an article about Remy and her collectible dolls. There's a picture of her holding Lily.

"That's it! That's the doll!" I shout. "But when is that dated? She claims she got Lily when Mr. Beasley was killed a couple of days ago. But there she is with her in a magazine."

"She got Lily six months ago."

Now it's *my* turn to gasp. "She lied to me!"

16

I'm still processing the fact Remy lied to me about where she was the night of Mr. Beasley's murder when Tom texts me to tell me my bus is ready.

"I should get back to Tom's place," I tell Wendy.

"What are you going to do about Remy?" she asks.

"I'm not sure yet."

"Do you think she lied because she killed Mr. Beasley?"

"Why else would she lie about where she was? Why not tell me the truth but say she didn't kill him?" I point out.

"I don't know," Wendy shakes her head.

"She also told me that Dustin Holmes' family insists that the doll belongs to them."

"Dustin Holmes? The rich guy?" she asks.

"I guess. She told me his offices are in the financial district. I think I should talk to him too. Even though I know, Remy is lying. It couldn't hurt, right?"

"Just promise you'll be careful, Holly. I still feel uneasy about this," Wendy warns.

"I thought your uneasy feeling was about Mr. Beasley dying," I remind her.

"That was correct, wasn't it?" she points out.

"Are you sure you aren't just a nervous nelly?"

"Don't knock my premonitions!" she warns.

"Fair enough, you're right. I promise I'll be careful. What can this guy do to me in his office, anyway? I'm sure there are tons of people around. I only want to ask him about his family's so-called claim on this doll. I'll let you know what I find out. Thanks for the information about Remy, by the way!"

"Be careful, Holly!" she shouts again when I head out the door to pick up my bus.

While we drive to Dustin's office, Clara recounts their time at the garage. She and Mystery explain the people and cars who came and went. I'm only half listening because I'm still mulling over my conversation with Remy and the fact, she lied to me.

I searched for Dustin's office address and phone number on the internet and called his secretary to see if he was in. She insisted he was in meetings all day, but don't they all say that?

He's obviously not just going to let some stranger walk into his office and ask him about a murder and doll theft. I hope that by showing up in person, the secretary will take pity on me and let me see him.

When I arrive, there's no one at the front desk, anyway. The door immediately to the right of the desk bears the name *Dustin Holmes CEO.* "It's now or never," I whisper to myself. I think by not giving him the chance to prepare a story, I have a better chance of getting the truth from him. I tap on his door while opening it slowly.

A tall, thin man with short red hair and a beard sits in a cushy chair behind a massive mahogany desk. His feet are propped on the desk, while talking on the phone. Remy was right. These offices are expensive. It even smells expensive. If expensive has a smell, that is.

Every detail appears arranged to convey loads of money. No detail was overlooked. From the artwork to the furniture, right down to the beverage cart in the corner.

I may not be able to estimate the exact value of the artwork or the furniture other than *pricey*, but as a bartender, I know everything on the beverage cart, from the liquor to the chunky, artful decanters, down to the glassware are extremely high end.

There are thousands of dollars sitting on that beverage cart alone. Why would someone like this insist that a collectible doll belongs in his family? Perhaps it's a matter of family pride, but it certainly isn't the money.

"Mr. Holmes?" I ask softly.

"I gotta go," he says to whoever is on the phone, hanging up with a flourish. He pops up from his chair like a jumping bean. "Hello there! Please call me Dustin!" he booms, his hand outstretched in greeting. I extend my hand which he shakes vigorously.

"I'm so sorry to barge in unannounced, but I have a few quick questions for you. I'm Holly Daniel," I tell him. "Paranormal Private Investigator."

"Greetings, Holly Daniel, Paranormal Private Investigator! How are you?"

"I'm well. How are you?" He seems awfully happy to see a stranger he wasn't expecting.

"I'm fabulous! It's a beautiful day, isn't it?" he gushes.

You know how some people seem genuinely happy. They make you feel good just being around them? It's not this guy.

It's contrived. His expensive suit, the designer office decor, and the Mr. Rodgers persona feel fake. But maybe it's just me. Besides, what does it matter? I'm just here to ask him about the Bebe Mothereau.

"Have a seat, Holly; what can I do for you?" he grins at me, but I notice the smile doesn't reach his eyes.

"I'm investigating the murder of Mr. Beasley, the doll museum owner."

"Such a tragedy," he replies.

"Yes, the last time I saw him, he told me he was expecting an expensive collectible doll from Denver. A signed copy of a Bebe Mothereau."

Dustin pinches his lips together. "What would that have to do with me?" he asks.

"I'm told that while it came from a collector in Denver, you believe it belongs to you."

He sighs. "That doll was in my family for generations until the collector you just mentioned stole it."

"Stole it?"

"Yes. Stole it."

"That's a serious accusation."

"Oh, it's not an accusation; it's a fact. He stole the doll from my family; besides, from what I hear, it's missing again. Stolen by the person who killed Mr. Beasley, I assume."

"How did the collector in Denver steal it?"

"It's a long story, but through a series of marriages, divorces, death, you know how it goes, the doll ended up with Vincent Whelan. When I reminded him it belonged in my family, he insisted it was his. Then he has the audacity to loan it out to Beasley, as if it's his to loan out in the first place."

"I understand the doll is quite valuable," I point out.

"I don't care what it's worth," he snaps, indicating the opulence in his office. "It's a matter of family pride. I assure you; I don't value the doll for the money. I value it because it belongs in my family."

"I see. Can I ask you where you were when Mr. Beasley was killed?"

"I was in Iowa at my grandmother's funeral," he says, opening his desk drawer and taking out a memorial card he hands me.

I feel guilty for interrogating a man who had just buried his grandmother.

"I'm sorry for your loss," I tell him.

"Thank you. I had hoped to be able to tell her I got the doll back, but alas, now it's in the hands of yet another thief. Possibly a murderer," he shudders.

We're both startled to hear arguing outside the office door. When Sheriff Mack bursts in, I leap up from the chair I'm so surprised. I notice, however, that Dustin doesn't seem that surprised.

"What are you doing here?" I ask Sheriff Mack.

"What am *I* doing here? What are *you* doing here?" he says.

"I'm investigating Mr. Beasley's murder."

"On whose authority?" he asks.

"I am a licensed private investigator, as you very well know."

"You're also a person of interest in the murder and doll theft, in case you've forgotten!" He chastises me.

"You're a person of interest?" Dustin asks, surprised.

I smile back.

"I haven't forgotten!" I respond through clenched teeth.

"Dustin Holmes, you're under arrest," the sheriff says.

Whoa! He's arresting him? Did Dustin Holmes kill Mr. Beasley? Could it be this easy? But if he's arresting him for killing Mr. Beasley, why did he remind me I'm a person of interest? I'm confused.

"You're under arrest for failing to make child support payments," Sheriff Mack tells him.

Child support? What the heck?

"Do we have to do this now?" Dustin asks.

"Oh gosh, I'm sorry, is this a bad time?" the sheriff retorts.

"Well, I do have an appointment after this one..." one look at the sheriff's face, and Dustin shuts up. I can't believe he thought Sheriff Mack was serious about there being a more convenient time.

Deputy Owens, the same deputy who was so eager to haul me to jail after Mr. Beasley was killed, handcuffs Dustin, then nods at me as he's leading him out of his office. Like we're old acquaintances or something.

"Cecelia, call my lawyer!" Dustin barks at his secretary.

"Already on it!" she responds. I notice he dropped the 'isn't this a great day' shtick. I knew he was phony. Why is he getting arrested for failing to pay his child support? With his money? What a jerk.

While Sheriff Mack is busy talking to his other deputy, I attempt to sneak out unnoticed. Obviously, my interview with Dustin is over. For now, anyway.

"Where do you think you're going?" Sheriff Mack growls as I try to slide past him.

"I was just leaving. Now that you've arrested my suspect."

"*Your* suspect?" he laughs.

"He should be your suspect, too, you know!" I retort.

"Why is that?" he asks.

"Remy Cashmore told me that his family thinks the stolen doll belongs to them and that the collector in Denver stole it from him."

"You don't say. Why were you talking to Remy? Is she a friend of yours?"

"No, if you must know, I went there to ask if she knew anything about Mr. Beasley and the doll."

"What made you think she would?" Sheriff Mack asks.

"Because Pa--" I cut myself short. I'm revealing too much here.

"So that's what you were doing that night," he muses. "You're getting around."

"Someone has to clear my name!"

"*We* are doing everything we can to solve this case," he says.

"Good to know!" I tell him as I march out the door with whatever dignity I have left.

17

When I get back to the bus, Clara and Mystery are bursting to tell me about the man who law enforcement lead from the building in handcuffs. Clara points out that she saw our *handsome* friend, Sheriff Mack. She's never letting this go.

"The man they arrested was Dustin Holmes, the guy I was here to question," I tell them.

"They already arrested him for murder?" Clara asks. "That was easy. Now you're off the hook!"

"They arrested him for failing to pay his child support, not murder," I tell her, shaking my head.

"Child support?" she yelps. "But you said he was rich!"

"He is, so I don't know what the problem is."

"Did you ask him where he was when Mr. Beasley was killed?" Mystery says.

"I did. He said he was at his grandmother's funeral."

"Oh gosh, that's too bad. Still, he should pay his child support," Clara points out. "Where to next? Can we go somewhere else? We don't have to go home yet, do we?"

"Now that you mention it, I'm craving a chocolate mint cupcake," I tell her.

"Yay! We're going to the bakery!" she cheers.

This time there's a parking spot directly in front of Sol Conceptions that I slide into. Walking into Juliet's bakery, I accidentally overhear what I'm sure are two people discussing the possessed killer doll on the loose in Glenwood.

I guess that's better than them whispering about how I'm a suspect, but I realize what an uphill battle it will be to discover the real killer.

"Holly!" Juliet shouts as I walk in the door.

"Hi Juliet! I'm craving a mint chocolate cupcake. Do you have any?"

"I made some fresh this morning!" she says. "How goes the investigation?"

"I just watched Dustin Holmes get arrested, if that's any indication," I sigh.

"Dustin killed Mr. Beasley?"

"No, unfortunately, that's what I thought at first, too. Well, actually, he may have killed him. I don't know. He has an alibi, though."

"But they still arrested him for murder?" she presses.

"No, they arrested him for failure to pay child support."

"Seriously? But he's rich!"

"I know!" I throw my hands in the air.

"What a jerk," she announces.

"Yep. You'll never believe this. I just heard the couple outside talking about a possessed doll!"

"Oh Miss Holly, the whole town has been talking about it. There are two camps. The part that thinks you killed him and the part that makes up even wilder stories than that involving poltergeist-possessed dolls. You won't believe the number of people who are insisting *they* saw the doll, or their neighbor's cousin's dentist saw the doll running down the street, antagonizing a squirrel, or stealing grapes at the grocery store."

"This town has quite the imagination, doesn't it?" I acknowledge.

"Wendy filled me in on what happened to you last night on Red Mountain. Are you sure you're okay?"

"I'm fine." I wave my hand dismissively. "Tom put a new bolt on this morning, so I don't have to worry about that again. Thanks for telling the Sheriff's Department where to find me, by the way."

"We were so worried!" she exclaims.

"I know, I know. There was no cell service out there, otherwise I swear you and Wendy would have been the first that I called."

"Not Sheriff Mack?" she teases.

"It wouldn't have occurred to me!" I insist.

"Okay, whatever you say. I'm just glad he could rescue you again."

"Did Wendy also tell you I talked to Remy Cashmore this morning *and* found she lied about where she was when Mr. Beasley died.?"

"She mentioned that as well. So what next? Will you confront Remy about it? Wendy also said you think the stolen doll is in a lockbox in her house?"

"It just fits," I tell her. "There's a lockbox next to a new display case. A very nice display case, I might add. One that would be perfect for a limited edition, autographed doll. She also seemed nervous that I was in there. Told me I was upsetting the dolls and ushered me back out into the living room."

"Whatever you do, be careful. Wendy senses something dark on the horizon and we both know not to ignore her premonitions."

"I know, she warned me too," I nod my head. "There's one more stop I want to make today, so I'll be on my way. But thanks for the cupcake!"

"Call us if you need help!" Juliet lectures as I head out the door. "I mean it!"

18

I wander the museum parking lot, waiting for Bianca to appear. I hope the poltergeists aren't causing her too much grief. The yellow crime scene tape is gone, so the Sheriff's Department must have finished its investigation at the museum. I wish they'd complete their *entire* investigation and figure out who really killed Mr. Beasley.

"Holly! You came back!" Bianca shouts with glee as she appears in front of me.

"I'm sorry I haven't been around lately; I've been very busy today investigating the case." I point in the museum's direction.

"I wish I could be more help. I should have paid closer attention that night when I saw the person leaving."

"That's okay; how could you have known?'

"Have you found any new evidence, or does the sheriff still think you did it?" she asks.

"I went to Remy Cashmore's house to talk to her because I heard she's a rival doll collector and would be eager to get her hands on the Bebe Mothereau."

"Is she the really short lady with the wild eyebrows?" Bianca giggles.

"Yes!" I laugh.

"What's she like in person?" she asks.

"Her house is full of dolls! She's actually very nice. Eccentric. But nice."

"Somehow, that doesn't surprise me. Do you think she could have killed Mr. Beasley? Even though she's a nice lady?"

"I think it's possible that she was so determined to get that doll she may have accidentally killed Mr. Beasley in the process." I speculate. "There's a lockbox in a room in her house that I think the doll is in, but she interrupted me before I could examine it closer."

"You should be careful! She could be a killer!" Bianca warns.

"I know. Believe me, I thought about that when I was there. I also just found out that she lied about her alibi for the night of the murder."

"Are you going to ask her why she lied?" she asks, her expression wide-eyed.

"I'm still working on that."

"Did you talk to anyone else?"

"I also talked to Dustin Holmes," I tell her.

"That rich guy?"

"Yep. His family claims that the doll rightfully belongs to them. They say that the collector in Denver stole it, and they want it back."

"Do you think *he'd* kill to get it? It's worth a lot of money," she reminds me.

"I don't think he's as concerned about the money. I think he's more focused on family honor. The problem is, I didn't get very far in the interview."

"How come? Did he throw you out?"

"No, he got arrested," I divulge.

"For murder?" she gasps.

"No, that's what I was hoping at first, too. The sheriff arrested him for failing to pay child support."

Bianca's face grows dark. "You're kidding!"

"Nope."

"That jerk isn't paying child support?" she asks.

"Not according to the Sheriff's Department."

"That makes me so mad!" she practically spits.

I know from what Bianca has told me, her mom struggled as a single parent, so I don't blame her for being so upset.

"Well, I really should get home now. I need to decide what I should do next, but I wanted to stop by and say hello," I tell her.

"Okay, cool, see you later," she says right before she vanishes. That's something I'll never understand about ghosts. Where do they go when they disappear like that? I asked Clara, but she claims even she doesn't know.

19

After further pondering my experience with Remy I realize I have to confront her about her lie. I think she killed Mr. Beasley and stole the doll. Okay, so I admit, it's more of a gut feeling than actual evidence, but I'm following up on it.

I worry the sheriff would just laugh at me, but if I confront Remy about her lie, I bet she'll try to hide the doll elsewhere, then Sheriff Mack can move in on her.

When I arrive at the house, I notice that the lawnmowing doll is lying on her side. That's odd. I hardly think Remy would leave her like that if she knew.

What is wrong with me? I'm here to confront her on her alibi, yet I'm worried about one of her lawn ornaments being out of place. Get a grip, Holly. As I approach the front door I see that not only is the inside door open, but the screen door is also ajar.

"Remy?" I call through the opening. "Excuse me, Remy?" I knock softly, but still no response. I slowly open the screen door, peering into her house, only to see feet sticking out from behind a chair.

What is it with me and feet lately? I burst inside to find an unconscious Remy on the ground. Her teacup lying on the floor next to her.

"Remy!" I shout, leaning down to feel for a pulse. It's there, but it's faint. I pull my phone from my pocket so fast I nearly drop it. I call 911 to tell them there's a medical emergency at

Remy Cashmore's house. Then I have to dash back outside to check the address because I still don't know it.

They undoubtedly wouldn't appreciate me referring to it as "that dollhouse." I urge them to hurry as I race back inside to check on her. I don't see any blood. Did she have a heart attack? I desperately wish I'd taken that first aid class I keep meaning to take.

Although I don't know what to do when there are no apparent signs of trauma. Her heart is beating so I don't think she needs CPR. This is awful. My own heart is beating so fast I'm sure it will jump from my chest at any second.

Then the most horrible thought in the world hits me. It's so bad I nearly dismiss it. I stare at Remy and then down the hall, toward the room with the lockbox. Then back at Remy. I reach down again. She still has a faint pulse. I stare down the hall one more time.

When I hear the ambulance siren, I decide it's now or never. I run to the room I was in before. The door to the empty lockbox is open. But the display case where I'm sure she planned to put the stolen doll is also still empty.

I frantically case the room for the Bebe Mothereau. It has to be here somewhere, but where? I check the closet and pull open drawers as the sirens grow closer.

I'm trying not to panic but I have to find that doll! When they pull up in front of the house, I run from the room, straight into Sheriff Mack. He doesn't flinch, but I fall on my butt.

"Sheriff!" I exclaim.

"Ms. Daniel," he growls.

"Remy!" I wheeze, pointing to the living room.

"I saw her," he says as paramedics enter the house. "What are you doing here?"

"Well, I..." Rats. What am I doing here? "Errrrr." Why can't I think of a perfect excuse? "I called 911!" Oh, that's brilliant Holly.

"I know that. I also know that within a matter of days, I've caught you red-handed at two crime scenes. What are you doing in here? What are you looking for?"

"This is a crime scene?" I gulp. "I thought she had a heart attack."

"Unless and until we know differently, I'm treating this as a crime scene."

If I hadn't realized earlier how awful this looks for me, I do now. "What do you think happened to Remy?" I ask. Please say heart attack! Stroke! Fainting spell! Anything but murder.

"I don't *know* what happened to her. You still haven't answered my question. Why are you here?"

I'm still sitting on the ground, peering up at the sheriff, and I feel so dumb. I start to get up, but he puts a firm hand on my shoulder, forcing me to stay in this vulnerable position.

He really knows how to make a person nervous. I sigh in resignation. I might as well tell him the truth since I can't seem to come up with a lie I think he'll believe.

"I talked to Remy earlier about Mr. Beasley and the missing doll. She lied to me when I asked her where she was when he died, but I only just discovered that. I came back here to conf--, I mean, ask her about it." He raises an eyebrow at my mistake with the word *confront*. "I thought if I asked her why she lied, she would admit that she stole the doll and killed Mr. Beasley."

"Then what?" he glares at me.

"Then I was going to call you right away! I swear!"

"Why didn't you call me before?"

"I thought you would say I didn't have enough evidence?"

"You still should have called me beforehand. What were you thinking, coming here alone, anyway? Especially if you're convinced she killed Mr. Beasley!"

"Convinced might be a strong word."

He purses his lips at me.

"More like a solid hunch," I offer. I'm just making this worse.

"Can I get up now?"

He reaches his hand down, pulling me up like I weigh nothing, while I dust off my pants.

"Sheriff!" we hear the EMTs call out.

Please, please, please let her be alive.

"Yep!" he answers as we walk back into the living room.

The paramedics are shocked to see me. "We're headed to the hospital now."

"Any idea what happened?" Sheriff Mack asks.

"Not sure. Possibly poison?"

"Poison!" I exclaim in horror.

The sheriff turns to me. "Holly Daniel, you're under arrest."

20

"**Y**ou're arresting me?" I shout. "You've got to be kidding."

"You know that you're a person of interest in Mr. Beasley's murder, and now I find you alone with an unconscious person who's also connected to the doll museum. If I don't take you in for questioning, I'll be in big trouble at the station."

"So, you're *not* arresting me?"

"I'm bringing you in for questioning."

"Am I under arrest or not?"

"I'm detaining you."

"Why won't you answer me? Why are you so frustrating?"

"Do you *want* me to arrest you?" he snaps.

"Of course not!"

"Then come with me to the station and answer some questions."

"Fine," I grumble. "Hang on, how will I get back here?"

He sighs as if I'm the most exasperating person he's ever met. Good. I hope I drive him crazy.

"Do you promise to follow me to my office?"

"I guess," I mumble.

"No, not, *I guess*. Promise me you won't take off."

"Where would I go anyway?"

"I think you might run me around town just to irritate me."

He's got me there.

"I promise I will follow you to the station."

"Fine, let's go," he demands, waving his hand toward the door.

I follow him to the Sheriff's Department, then dutifully up the steps and into the building. This feels so official it makes me nauseous.

Besides, I'm worried about Remy. She may be a bit weird, but she was perfectly lovely to me at her house.

I hope she's okay, even if she killed Mr. Beasley and stole the doll. What if it wasn't a heart attack? But what else could it be? I didn't see any blood or injuries, so I don't think anyone hit her or stabbed her.

Perhaps she fell and smacked her head, but I couldn't tell. Although, that wouldn't explain why the lockbox was empty.

Could it really be poison? I follow the sheriff wordlessly down the hallway, where he opens a door, then points at a chair in front of a steel table.

"Sit!" he demands.

I sit down, trying to come up with a witty retort but I can't think of one.

I jump when he slams the door shut and leaves. What now? Is he coming back? Does he want me to sit here and sweat it out?

After what seems like hours, he returns with a file folder and a notebook. I cringe at the obnoxious noise the chair makes scraping across the floor.

He plops down in the chair, slamming the file and notebook on the table, so I jump again. Does he enjoy rattling me or what?

"Why don't you explain to me again what you were doing at Remy's house."

I don't know why he wants the story again, but I humor him. I explain I went there earlier in the week to talk to her about Mr. Beasley and the missing doll. I also remind him I was sure the missing doll was in the lockbox, but now it's empty.

"Why are you sure the doll was in the lockbox?" he asks.

"I think she killed Mr. Beasley to get the doll. But if it was in the lockbox, I don't know where it is now." I hold my hands up and shrug. I'm out of answers. But then it hits me. "Wait! What if she felt so guilty over killing Mr. Beasley that she tried to kill herself?"

"With what?" the sheriff asks.

"I don't know. It was just a suggestion!" This is so frustrating.

"A suggestion to throw us off the real killer's trail?" he asks.

"You mean me!" I snap.

"I found you with Mr. Beasley *and* Remy," he reminds me.

"How is she, by the way? Have you heard anything?"

"I have not."

He stares at me silently for what must have been at least a minute. I know he's hoping by not saying anything, I'll get uncomfortable and talk. Joke's on him. I don't know what more to say. We glare at each for a while longer.

Eventually, he pulls a picture of a young woman from the file folder.

"Ashley!" I exclaim.

"Her name is Abby," he corrects me.

"Oh, oops, Abby. Did you ask her to confirm my alibi? She was working the check-in desk that night."

"She left for vacation the next day, so no, I haven't been able to confirm your alibi."

"Oh. Well, I know when she gets back she'll tell you I was there." I offer hopefully. Why can't I get a break here?

He refuses to look away as he slides the photo back into the file folder. I want to ask for a glass of water to break the tension but I'm sure he'll say no anyway.

"It could help both of us if you would just share what you know about the investigation. You were at Dustin Holmes' office when I arrested him. What lead you there?" he asks.

"Remy told me that his family swears the doll belongs to them."

"Yes, you mentioned that before," he mumbles, as I watch him scribble some notes. "I assume you asked him where he was when Beasley was killed?"

"I did."

"And?" I can tell he's still frustrated with me. I admit I enjoy poking at him.

"He was at his grandmother's funeral in Iowa."

"Did you get proof?"

"He gave me the memorial card."

"How is that proof?"

"I don't know! I took it as proof. Should I have pressed him on it? His grandma died!"

"This is a murder investigation. It's not a time to be delicate. Did you ask him for a copy of his plane ticket? A hotel or car rental receipt?"

"No, I didn't think about that."

He rolls his eyes. I'm sure he thinks that I'm just some dumb amateur. Yes, I am an amateur, but I don't think I'm dumb. Just inexperienced.

"Hey, you arrested him before I could question him further," I retort.

"You're not helping your case," he explains.

There's a sharp rap on the door. A deputy enters, whispers in Sheriff Mack's ear, glances at me with disdain, then leaves. In an infuriatingly calm way, he tells me, "Remy Cashmore was poisoned."

"Poisoned!" I shriek. "Someone poisoned her?" I remember there was only one cup, though. Maybe she did try to kill herself. But then where is the doll? Did she ever have the doll? So many questions!

"She's still alive, though?" I'm almost afraid to ask.

"She's in a coma. We can't question her until she wakes up. *If* she wakes up."

I remember the shoe in my pocket. Maybe this will prove to Sheriff Mack that I'm willing to cooperate. "I found this in the museum parking lot the night Mr. Beasley was killed."

"You took evidence from a crime scene?"

"Oh, uh, I don't really see it like that."

"I'm sure you don't. Let me look at it." He holds his hand out. Now I hesitate to hand it over. I've grown rather attached to it. "I said let me see it!"

"Okay, here. I want it back, though."

"I'll decide if and when you get it back."

He looks it over thoughtfully. "You found this in the parking lot?"

"Yes."

"Where in the parking lot?"

"It was by my bus."

"Did you find it before or after you entered the museum?" He stares me down as if he can intimidate me into giving him better answers.

"After. I didn't notice it before."

"It's just a tiny shoe," he points out.

"I know. I think it belongs to a doll."

"Which doll?" he sighs.

"I don't know for sure. It could be any doll, but I wonder if it belongs to the missing doll."

He turns it over and looks at it again. "I suppose you can keep it." When he hands it back to me, I carefully return it to back in my pocket. I don't know why, but I feel like it's important. I won't share that thought with him, though.

"Juliet told me she sensed negative energy in it." The moment I say that out loud, I regret it. It sounds so lame out of context

"Did she now?" he responds, folding his hands together and staring at me.

"Oh, my gosh! I just remembered something else!" I exclaim.

"Do tell," he says with a steely eyed glare.

Why does he have to be so sarcastic? I'm serious here.

"After I left Remy's house..." he opens his mouth to ask the question, "the first time." I answer for him. "Clara was in the bus waiting for me--"

"Why was Clara in the bus?" he interrupts.

"She and Mystery like to go for rides."

He looks at me like he can't believe he's hearing this. Welcome to my world, pal.

"Anyway," I continue, "Clara told me she saw a tall man sneaking around outside Remy's house."

"What did he look like? What was he doing?" he asks, the agitation really beginning to show now.

"She said he was tall and that he was sneaking around." I cringe at how that sounds.

"You already said that," he reminds me.

"Sorry, that's all I have."

"Here's what I'll do. You wait here, and I'll let my deputies know that your 143-year-old roommate told you about a tall man sneaking around Remy's house."

My cheeks flush. "You don't have to be so grumpy. I'm trying to help here, you know!"

"The way you can help is to get out of my way and let me solve this case. Stop running off, without backup, to question people you think killed Mr. Beasley." He takes a deep breath. "I think we're done here," he announces suddenly, placing the notebook inside the file folder and closing it before I can see what else is in there.

"Does that mean I can go?" I ask.

"You can go, but the usual applies--"

"Don't leave town!" I respond sarcastically.

"I can put you in a holding cell right now if you prefer," he grunts.

"Nope! I'm good!" I assure him. "I won't leave town."

"If you get any more evidence that you think points to the killer, you let me know first!" he lectures.

"Whatever you say, Sheriff," I mumble on my way out the door.

"Holly, one more thing."

It always surprises me, the rare times he calls me Holly instead of Ms. Daniel. I pause, but I won't to turn around. I refuse to give him the satisfaction of looking at him while he lectures me on whatever he's about to lecture me on.

"You may want to check into Dustin Holmes' financials."

I spin around to stare at him, I'm so shocked he gave me a tip rather than scolding me about something. But then continues to gather his things as if he didn't say a word.

I could point out that he clearly doesn't see me as the killer, but I decide to quit while I'm ahead this time.

21

Now that I'm out of prison, so to speak, I drive to the museum hoping Bianca will appear. I want to ask her about the shoe to see if she recognizes it. I'm a little surprised however, to see her and one of the poltergeists talking outside.

Great! I can talk to both of them. But when I pull into a parking spot, and get out of the bus, Bianca is still there, yet the poltergeist has disappeared.

"Hey!" I shout to her. "Where did he go?"

"Danny?" she asks.

"Is that his name?" I just realized I never got his name. He didn't exactly offer it.

"Yeah, he's such a jerk." She scowls.

"Where did he go?"

"Back to the museum? He can go just about anywhere, you know."

I nod my head. "Yeah, I realize that."

"I wanted to talk to him about the night Mr. Beasley was killed."

"He knows nothing!" she snaps.

"Okay." I hold my hands up. "I was just wondering." Who knew spirits could be so touchy?

"Sorry about that. Those guys always put me in a bad mood."

"Do they pick on you?"

"Unfortunately, yes"

"I hate that."

She looks surprised. "Do you get bullied?" she asks

"Not like I used to. When I was in school, though, kids picked on me constantly."

"How come?"

"My lavender eyes." I point to them. "Also, my ability to talk to the dead."

"I think your eyes are pretty!" she seems shocked anyone would bully me for that.

"Thanks. I don't know what it is with kids, but anytime a person is the least bit different, they torment them, don't they?"

"My mom was the town drunk, and my dad was non-existent, so they bullied me over that."

"Sadly, I'm not surprised." I tell her.

"You've always been able to talk to ghosts?"

"My parents first noticed when I was about six years old. I talked to my friend's dead grandma."

"Why did you tell other kids you could see ghosts if they picked on you for it?"

"I didn't tell them, but when I was in foster care, I slipped a few times, and they made fun of me for having imaginary friends."

"But they weren't imaginary!" she exclaims.

"Nope!"

"What did you do after that?"

I wince. "I pretended I didn't see the ghosts."

"That must have been hard," she points out.

"It was, and over the years, I got angrier and angrier. Then I got fired from my job in Florida, my husband died, and I blamed others for everything that had happened to me. Then I moved here."

"You seem pretty nice to me."

"I've met some good people here who didn't just tiptoe around my destructive behavior. They weren't mean to me about it, but they pointed out in a loving, yet firm way that I needed a serious attitude adjustment. I like to think I'm getting better at being a nice person now."

"That's cool that you made friends here. Am I your friend?" she asks hopefully.

"I like to think so," I respond.

She smiles wistfully.

"Hey, I found something the night Mr. Beasley was killed."

"What?" she snaps.

"Don't worry. I don't even know if it's relevant, but I thought I'd ask you, anyway."

"Why?"

Why is she so moody? "I figured you might know. I'm not blaming you for anything, if that's what you're thinking."

"Oh. Okay. Sorry again, it's just that those poltergeists have me worked up. *They* always want to blame stuff on me."

"Why would the poltergeists blame you?"

"You know how they are. They aren't happy unless they're causing trouble."

"Okay, well, this is what I found." I pull the shoe from my pocket, holding it out to her. "Do you know which doll this belongs to?"

Bianca shudders.

"What?"

"It belongs to *that* doll!" She backs up. "The expensive doll from Denver."

"The missing doll? You're sure the shoe is from the stolen doll?"

She nods her head vigorously.

"Why are you so nervous?" I ask.

"Everyone says the doll is possessed by a poltergeist! They think it killed Mr. Beasley!"

I wonder why a ghost is afraid of a possessed doll, but I don't press her on it.

"You should be careful carrying it around like that. You should leave it here!"

I look around. "Where would I leave it? The museum is locked! There's nowhere to put it."

"Just throw it on the ground!" she insists, growing increasingly agitated.

"It belongs to a $20,000 doll and might be the key to solving the mystery," I point out.

"I'm telling you right now that shoe and the doll are trouble. Mark my words!" she says ominously before disappearing into thin air.

"Bianca!" I call out. "Come back!"

22

Like I predicted, Clara and Mystery were worried about me. Well, Clara was worried. Mystery is a cat, so she was mostly worried about any drama that might interfere with her next nap. But at least Clara genuinely worries about me.

I sit with them much like I did Wendy and Juliet while giving them the rundown of the day's events. Clara said she saw the story about Remy on the news and the latest update is that she's still in a coma and they don't know if she'll make it.

I desperately hope she regains consciousness soon because I need to know who did this to her. Was the doll in the lockbox? If so, where is it now?

Clara and Mystery whisper to each other.

"What are talking about? Why are you whispering?" I ask.

"Mystery overheard something that might be important." Clara explains.

"Where did you overhear anything? You can't leave here." I remind her.

"In the bus, the other day at Tom's shop."

"Oh, that's right. With everything that has happened, that feels like it was a lifetime ago. All right Mystery, spit it out. What did you overhear?"

"Do you still think Dustin Holmes could have killed Mr. Beasley?" she asks.

That's an odd question, but I'll bite.

"I'm not convinced that he did. He was at his grandmother's funeral when Beasley died, but why do you ask? I haven't completely ruled him out, if that's what you're wondering. I tried to talk to him the other day about it, but Sheriff Mack had to come in and arrest for not paying child support."

"Uhhh, okay." Mystery squints at me. "Anyway, his cousin works at Tom's shop," she tells me.

I wait for her to continue, but she doesn't. "And?" I snap. She could be in contention with Sheriff Mack for the most annoying, errr, being.

"Oh, sorry about that," Mystery shakes herself out. "I was just daydreaming about my next nap there. Anyway, I heard the cousin talking about the funeral in Iowa. The one for the grandmother."

"Yes!" I shout. "Did he say if Dustin was there?"

"I dont know, it's not like I could ask him."

"Did he say anything else?"

"He said the only reason he went was that he was hoping the old lady had left him some money."

"Well, did she?" I press.

"Nope." Mystery shakes her head.

"Then what did she do with it?"

"He said she left it to some rabbit charity."

"Rabbits?" I ask.

"Rabbits," Mystery confirms. "Personally, I've always thought rabbits were weird."

I know I'll regret this. "Why do you think rabbits are weird?"

"Those pink eyes!" Mystery meows.

"What's wrong with pink eyes?" Clara asks. "I think pink eyes would be pretty. Like your lavender ones," she nods at me.

"What if rabbits think your green eyes are weird," I tell Mystery. Then I ask myself why we're having this conversation in the first place. "How does any of this help me determine who killed Mr. Beasley?"

"Don't forget Remy!" Clara reminds me.

"That too. How does this help me?"

Mystery glares at me like I'm an imbecile. "You ask the cousin if Dustin Holmes was at the funeral. If he wasn't, you know he lied about his alibi, and you can confront him." She shakes her head. "Do I have to do all the work around here? Now if you'll excuse me, there's a sunbeam somewhere with my name on it."

I focus on Clara. "Why didn't I think of that?"

23

"Hey there Holly!" Tom says when I pull into the parking lot of his shop. "Please tell me that bolt didn't fall out of the alternator again."

"Nothing like that thankfully. I'm here to see Bernie Holmes. Is he working today?"

"He sure is." He shouts, "Hey Bernie! C'mere! Someone wants to talk to you."

Bernie is tall like his cousin but that's where the resemblance ends. He has dark, longer hair that he keeps flipping over his shoulder. I wonder why he didn't go into the family business like Dustin.

"Hi, there, Bernie? I understand you're Dustin Holmes' cousin?"

"Yeah, who wants to know?"

"Holly is one of our customers," Tom explains before Bernie gets too worked up. "She drives the hot pink bus."

"Ohhhh yeah. That's an outstanding whip you've got."

"Oh, uh, thanks. I guess I can't really take credit for it, but it's grown on me."

"Can I help you with something?" he asks.

"First, I'm very sorry about your grandmother. I understand she passed away recently?"

"Yeah, but she left her fortune to a rabbit rescue!" Bernie snorts.

"Yes, I heard that too."

"Why are you interested in my grandma? Did she owe you money? Like I said, everything went to charity."

"Oh, no, it's nothing like that. Was your cousin Dustin at the funeral?"

"Why are you asking about him? Does *he* owe you money?" he frowns.

What is the deal with this family and money?

"No, he doesn't owe me money either. I just wondered if he was at the funeral."

"I have to tell you, lady, that seems like a really weird thing to be asking a stranger. What do you care?"

"Ohhh, wait a sec. You must be dating him!" Bernie exclaims.

"Dating him? No, I-- um, yes, we're dating. He stood me up last weekend and he told me he was at his grandmother's funeral, but I think he's cheating on me!" Wow, how did I come up with that one? Maybe I'm not as bad at this as I think sometimes.

Bernie laughs. "Yeah, I knew it must be something like that. Anyway, do not tell him you got this from me."

"Not a word! I promise!" I make a zipping motion across my lips.

"Dustin hasn't spoken to our grandmother in years. No way would he go to her funeral. When I told him she gave her money away, he said 'that figures.' So, to answer your question, lady, no, he was not at the funeral." He shakes his finger knowingly at me. "I knew he was up to no good when he asked me for a copy of the memorial card."

So that explains that.

"I'd break up with him if I were you," he tells me.

"I'll break up with him today!" I exclaim. "What a tool."

"You got that right!" Bernie tells me.

So, what do you know? Both suspects lied about their alibis. But which one killed Mr. Beasley and which one has the doll?

24

J ust as I get ready to head for Dustin's office my stomach
yells at me for neglecting it since breakfast.

I'll grab a quick breakfast at the food truck across the street,
then I'm going to see Dustin I tell myself.

Sammies Sammiches is one of the most popular places in
Glenwood to grab a quick bite so I consider myself lucky when
I find only a couple of people in line.

The order taker jots down my request - a scrambled egg
sandwich with sharp cheddar and bacon on multi-grain bread
- then she disappears into the food truck.

While I wait I take the shoe from my pocket to study it some
more. How can something so tiny cause such a fuss?

"Holly!" the cashier shouts, holding up my order bag.

Just as I take the bag, and turn to leave, a woman bulldozes
into me, sending the bag flying in one direction and the doll
shoe in another.

"Whoa!" I exclaim, scrambling to pick up my things.

The woman grabs my arm. "Oh my gosh, I'm so sorry! Are
you okay?"

"Uh, yeah, I'm fine," I tell her.

"I'm so sorry."

"It's okay!" I continue to assure her.

"Is your sandwich okay?"

"I'm sure it's fine. It's just a sandwich."

The old me would have complained and yelled at her to watch where she's going.

The new me only wants to retrieve my sandwich and the shoe and leave. What the heck was she doing, anyway? Jogging with her eyes closed?

I pick up the sandwich bag but nearly panic when I don't see the shoe. Oh, thank goodness, there it is, just a couple of feet away. I dash to the shoe and pick it up.

But when I stand up, I nearly run into a man planted in front of me. What the heck is happening today? This food truck is dangerous. Then I look up to see I almost ran smack into Dustin Holmes himself.

25

I hastily jam the doll shoe back in my pocket.

"Hello, Holly, is everything okay with your sandwich?" he asks.

"Yes, I'm sure it's fine," I respond. "Did you hit your head?" I point to a rather gruesome gash on his forehead. It has stitches, but the surrounding bruising will appear unsightly for a while.

"It was an unfortunate accident at the jailhouse," he says.

"Yikes, did you get into a fight?"

"No, nothing like that. They were processing my paperwork. When I turned to leave, a large file cabinet drawer flew out and hit me in the head. My lawyers are looking into suing."

No doubt.

"Hey, remember the other day when I was in your office?" I ask.

"Of course."

"Remember how you told me you were at your grandmother's funeral in Iowa?"

His face turns dark. "Why are you so interested in my whereabouts when Beasley was killed?" he asks through clenched teeth.

"I'm just trying to get to the bottom of this," I explain.

"The sheriff said you're the primary suspect. Are you trying to pin that guy's murder on someone else? Where were *you* when he was killed?" he asks.

"I was swimming laps," I state matter-of-factly.

"Oh. All right, fine, I was meeting with my lawyers. Here's their card. They can confirm my whereabouts."

"May I ask why you were meeting with your lawyers?" I say as innocent sounding as I can.

"Our child custody arrangements."

"Ah. Good to know. See your around," I wave to him while securing the card in my back pocket. Custody arrangements. Likely story.

<h1 style="text-align:center">26</h1>

What a couple of messed up days we've had. First Remy, then a trip to the jailhouse, then Bianca's meltdown over the doll shoe. It isn't any better this morning and I'm just getting started.

I know even before I contact them that Wendy and Juliet will be upset with me for not reaching out yesterday. I've been spinning from one crisis to another with this case and I'm worried what's next. I've barely had a moment to stop to catch my breath.

I might as well get this over with, I sigh. I text Wendy and Juliet from the park across the street from the food truck to see if they're available to meet me at the bookstore.

Wendy: Is it true Remy was killed by a possessed doll?

Me: No! At least I don't think so.

Juliet: Remy is dead?

Me: She isn't dead. Not yet anyway. Ugh. This is too much to text. Meet me at the bookstore.

Juliet: Someone in the bakery just said YOU killed Remy and got arrested yesterday! Why didn't you tell us you got arrested?!

Me: Just meet me at the bookstore.

When I finally arrive at the Looking Glass, they descend on me like it's a Black Friday sale at the electronics store. They fire off questions about Remy and my alleged arrest. Of course, they're furious I waited until now to contact them.

"Just calm down!" I urge. "It's been a crazy couple of days, and I swear I'm not withholding anything on purpose. This is the first moment that I've had the chance to fill you in."

"I'm already madder than a wet hen, so talk fast," Juliet demands as she leans in so close, I have to step back.

"What do we know so far?" Wendy asks. "Start from the beginning."

I take a deep breath as we settle in on the bookstore's comfortable couch. "Sheriff Mack is still the most annoying person I know." There. I said it. I've been wanting to complain about him all day.

Wendy and Juliet glower at me like they may just kill me at this point.

"The entire town is talking about a killer doll and your arrest for Remy's murder. On top of everything else, you failed to update your best friends. But that's what you lead with?" Wendy complains.

They're madder than I predicted. "Calm down and I'll explain everything. I swear. Hey, do you have any coffee?"

"Talk!" Juliet shouts.

"All right, all right, here's what happened." I fill them in on everything from finding Remy unconscious, to my trip to the police station, to learning that Remy was poisoned. Then they're shocked when I tell them that isn't everything and that I found out Dustin Holmes lied about his alibi too.

"Do they have any evidence of who could have poisoned her?"

"Not according to the Sheriff's Department," I explain.

"But according to you?" Juliet asks.

"I'm still certain that the stolen doll was in the lockbox at her house."

"Do you still think she killed Mr. Beasley, too?" Wendy asks.

"Yes."

"Did the poisoning change your mind?" Juliet asks.

"I don't know. How could she steal the doll and not kill him? But then who would want her dead unless they knew she had the doll and wanted it for themselves?"

"But you told us earlier you never saw what was in the lockbox, correct? You have to consider it may have been empty all along."

"You're right. It's certainly possible that Remy never had that doll. Or that she didn't kill Mr. Beasley. I don't know. I just have a gut feeling that the doll was in the lockbox, but now it's gone. I think whoever took it poisoned Remy to get it."

"Also!" I pull the shoe from my pocket. "Bianca confirmed the shoe belongs to the stolen doll."

"How do we know you can trust her?" Wendy asks. "I still have my doubts about her."

"What do you mean?" I respond.

"Ghosts can lie, right? Or can they? I don't know."

"Sure, they can lie. They basically maintain the same personality type in death that they had when they were living," I explain.

"So, if she was bad news while alive, then she could be bad news as a spirit, is what you're saying?" Wendy asks.

"Yes." I nod.

"Then I'm not sure you should trust this, Bianca."

"She seems fine to me." I insist. "We have similar backgrounds."

"Okay. Whatever you say." Wendy responds, but she looks skeptical.

"Why would Dustin lie to you about where he was when Mr. Beasley was killed?" Juliet asks. "What if he killed him to get the doll back for his family? If he's estranged from them, perhaps, he thought by getting the doll he'd be back in their good graces," Juliet suggests.

"I think it's possible," I tell her. "That's why I'll follow up with his lawyer today."

"Ladies, this has been fascinating, but I need to get back to the bakery!" Juliet announces, standing up from the couch.

"I should go too," I tell them. "I need to use your bathroom first, though."

"Do you really, or are you trying to sneak into another room?" Wendy asks in jest.

"Ha ha!" I tell her. "If you aren't hiding any stolen collectible dolls in the store you have nothing to worry about."

"Okay then, we'll be outside," Wendy says.

On my way back from the bathroom, I'm distracted by some new books. I thumb through them while reminding myself I already have a sky-high TBR pile and really don't need anymore, when I hear shouting and a loud crash.

I run to the entryway to see what happened. There's a crowd gathering on the sidewalk, some people are still shouting. I fling open the door to find a man on the ground clutching his knee and wailing.

There's a bent bike lying nearby on the sidewalk, with books strewn everywhere. He must have run into the books Wendy displays outside! Meanwhile, Wendy's face is pale, and several people are asking her if she's okay. Others ask the cyclist if he needs an ambulance.

"What the heck happened here?" I exclaim in horror.

"He tried to run me down!" Wendy points to the cyclist on the ground. "This is why you aren't supposed to ride on the sidewalk!" she scolds.

"Lady, I swear I was steering around you when I suddenly lost control. It was like something grabbed my handlebars and aimed the bike straight at you. I don't know what happened, but I promise I didn't do it on purpose."

"What do you mean something grabbed the handlebars? What a ridiculous excuse!" Juliet retorts.

"I bet it was the poltergeist doll!" a person from the crowd exclaims while the rest murmur their agreement.

Juliet leans over to whisper in my ear. "You don't think the doll could be responsible, do you?"

"No!" I insist. But something makes me wonder if it *could* happen. Wendy said she's never had trouble with poltergeists at the bookstore, and I don't see any spirits hovering, poltergeist or not.

But I know it's possible. Maybe not a rogue doll, but a poltergeist could have grabbed his handlebars, forcing him to wreck the bike.

The ambulance arrives within a matter of moments while the paramedics check over Wendy and the cyclist. Wendy's elbow is scraped from landing on the ground, but that's it. The cyclist's knee is badly injured, so they take him to the hospital for x-rays. While the crowd disperses, Wendy pulls me aside.

"Holly, you *must* be careful," she warns.

I nod my head. "I know."

"I don't think you do," she says. She's more serious than I've ever known her to be. "I sense a powerfully dark presence among us. Are you going anywhere else today?"

"Home, right now."

"Okay, good." She looks relieved.

"Although I'm working at the bar tonight," I add.

"Cancel," Juliet insists.

"Yes, cancel," Wendy urges.

"I can't! They're already short two people. Mr. Sinclair begged me to fill in."

By now, my friends know better than to think they can talk me out of something.

"Then call us when you get off work. We'll meet you," Wendy says.

"Don't you think that's a bit excessive, you guys?"

"No!" Wendy says so sharply that I jump. "We all need to be extra careful right now."

"Okay, okay, I got it. I'll see you, ladies, again tonight."

On the way home with my mind churns. My hands tremble a little more than I'd like. Too many dark things happening lately and I'm on edge about it. Finding Remy unconscious like that, knowing she could die, is almost too much to handle.

Then Wendy nearly gets run down by a cyclist. She could have been hurt. He could have been injured worse than he was. When he claimed that something forced him to steer in Wendy's direction it scared me.

I feel weird thinking that I hope the cyclist was lying about something grabbing his handlebars, and he was being careless instead. If he's telling the truth though and a dark element is wreaking havoc around town it could mean even more serious trouble for all of us.

27

The sky is ominous and dark. Like my mood. I don't remember the weather people predicting rain, but I can smell it. I park the car in the garage, and just as I get to the house, the first few raindrops splatter on my head. Clara and Mystery eagerly await to learn what I know from Tom's garage.

I explain everything that happened, but when I finish with Wendy's warning, I downplay it because I know what Clara's response will be. She quickly catches on, however.

"You should listen to Wendy!" she demands. "You need to stay home this evening. I don't want you at that bar."

"It's fine, Clara, besides Mr. Sinclair really needs me tonight. I'll be extra careful. I promise."

Of course, she doesn't believe me, but she drops it for now. Like Wendy and Juliet, she knows it's a losing argument.

It storms throughout the day. Heavy rain with black clouds, booming thunder, and brilliant bolts of lightning jag across the sky.

"Goodness gracious, this is unusual!" Clara exclaims repeatedly.

I call the lawyers on the card that Dustin gave me, and they confirm he advised them I'd call, and yes, he was meeting with them when Mr. Beasley was killed. They wouldn't, however, share *what* they met about.

Now I don't know what to think. The lawyers say he was with them, but why didn't he just say that to begin with? Why invent a story about his grandmother's funeral?

This whole thing is such a topsy-turvy mixed-up case I don't know what to think anymore. I call the hospital. They tell me Remy is still unconscious, so I can't move forward there. I'm at a complete loss.

"Holly! Come quick!" Clara shouts.

"What is it?"

"There's a spirit out front!"

"That's impossible." Clara and Mystery are the only spirits who live here. She told me that when I first met her. Although she said some of the previous owners were convinced that it had to be more than just her because she caused so much trouble.

I gaze out the window. It's so dark it's hard to make out anything but rain. "I don't see anything," I tell her.

"I swear, it was right there!" She points at the front yard just as a burst of lightning illuminates the sky, showing there's nothing there but the trees and water, which continues to pour down in torrents.

"What did it look like?"

"It was a young woman with long brown hair dressed in more modern clothing. I think she looks like that Bianca you keep talking about."

"But Bianca lives at the museum."

"All I know is what I saw. A young female ghost. There better not be someone trying to move in on my territory!" Clara exclaims, with her lips pursed.

"Maybe it was the storm playing tricks," I offer.

"It better be!" she scowls as another bolt of lightning arcs across the horizon. I squint at the yard, but I still don't see anything.

"Whatever it was, I have to get to work."

"What if I see something else out there?" she asks.

I know she's trying to convince me to stay home.

"You'll tell me all about it when I return."

"Remember, you said you'd call Wendy and Juliet when you're done at the bar!"

"I remember!" I tell her.

The drive to the hotel is nerve-wracking. Between the storm and everything else that happened today, even I admit I'm on edge. I really need to solve this thing before we all go bonkers.

While I sit at a red light on 6th Street, thunder booms so hard that the bus shakes. Then another burst of lightning illuminates the corner, and for one second, I swear I glimpse Bianca.

"What the heck?" I mutter. I do a double take, and then she or whoever it was is gone. I'm so tired, my mind must be playing tricks on me. I bet it's the power of suggestion.

Like when you decide you want to buy a certain kind of car and suddenly it's everywhere you turn. I'll be happy when I'm in bed tonight. Although if this thunder continues, I don't know how any of us will sleep.

I'm wiping a spilled drink off the bar when Fiona appears. I met her when I first started working here, and unfortunately, I ignored her at the time and regretted it. I don't ignore her anymore!

If she were alive, she'd be known as the town gossip. She knows everything that goes on with everybody. At least everything she hears in the hotel, anyway.

"People are talking about you again!" she exclaims, taking a seat at the bar.

"I know," I sigh. "I heard the gossip all night. Everyone thinks it's too much of a coincidence that the sheriff found me with two bodies in one week. Which isn't exactly fair because Remy is still alive. Besides, I didn't kill either of them. It was just super bad timing on my part. On top of everything else, Mr. Sinclair told me it might be a good idea if I stayed home until all of this blows over because I'm bad for business. I *should* have stayed home tonight, but I thought he needed me."

Fiona looks thoughtful. "Is there really a possessed doll on the lam?"

"You know, anything is possible here, but I have my doubts about a murderous, poltergeist-enhanced doll."

One benefit to being a spirit communicator is that spirits can't talk to another living being, so they have to keep my secrets. I catch Fiona up on the recent events, most of which she already knew about, but I can openly confide in her about how utterly defeated and confused I feel over everything that has happened. I'm sure I'm missing something. I just don't know what. I'm also nervous about Wendy's premonitions.

"So you're saying the possessed doll broke out of the lock-box, poisoned Remy, then took off for parts unknown?" she asks.

I laugh. "No, that's not what I'm saying! I think someone, a live human I mean, poisoned Remy and stole the doll."

"Got anybody specific in mind?"

"Not really," I sigh. "Dustin Holmes claims the doll belongs to his family. Although what could they want with a $20,000 collectible? He's filthy rich. It's not enough for him to kill over." I point out. "I understand family honor is invol--"

"Wait, did you say he's filthy rich?" she interrupts.

"I did. I've been in his office. They're loaded."

"Dustin Homes is broke!"

"What are you talking about?"

"He was in the bar on Monday night with his bankruptcy attorney. They were in the corner talking. It was all hush-hush. Except for me, of course," she boasts. "They say he squandered away the family fortune on gambling and cryptocurrency."

"Oh, my gosh." I smack my forehead.

"What?"

"When I was at his office the other day, they arrested him for failing to pay child support. At the time, I didn't understand how someone with that much money would let it get so bad that he got arrested. Sheriff Mack told me to check into Dustin's finances, but as usual, I dismissed it because it didn't fit in with the narrative I'd developed in my head. I feel so stupid now."

"$20,000 doesn't sound so paltry anymore, does it?" Fiona says.

28

W hat a miserable night. Everything that could go wrong did. I don't appreciate Mr. Sinclair chewing out by the manager for causing problems that I still say aren't my fault.

I can't help it if other people like to gossip. How could they think that I would kill Mr. Beasley or poison Remy? Then there's the rest who swear there's a poltergeist-infested doll running the streets of Glenwood. To top everything off it's still raining and It's later than I expected when I finish my shift at the bar.

I know Wendy and Juliet mean well, but they aren't helping with their premonitions of doom. Yes, I'm supposed to call them when I get off work so they can keep an eye on me, but I don't think even they realized it would be this late and I don't want to bother them. I'll just go home, pour a glass of wine, and a hot bath, then sink into a warm, lightly scented bubble concoction that Wendy created just for me, and soak my cares away.

It's eerie late at night especially in a storm. Even I'm getting the heebie-jeebies. Just as I start to unlock the VW door I drop my keys. Of course. Another thing I miss most about my old Subie is the electronic locks. I wonder what it would cost to have Tom install them on the bus? Is that even possible?

I bend down to get my keys when I hear squealing car tires. What idiot is racing around town this late at night in the middle of a rainstorm? They could kill someone, whoever they are. I look up to see if I can tell what kind of car they're driving, but I'm blinded by extra bright headlights pointed directly at me.

"Hey!" I protest, putting my hand up to my eyes to shield them from the glare. Now I get what they mean by a deer caught in the headlights. I can't see a thing, so by the time I realize the car is heading straight for me, it's too late. I fly through the air and land with a hard thud several feet away.

I just got hit by a car. Shouldn't this hurt more? Hang on a second. I didn't get *hit* by the car. I was pushed. Hard. Hard enough to knock me off my feet and send me flying. What the heck? I watch the car speed away, but I'm too stunned to register the type.

"Jerk!" I shout. Who could have pushed me like? I'm still confused. Then I see him and realize what just happened. I didn't get hit by the car because Sheriff Mack shoved me out of the way just in time. *He's* the one who got hit.

I leap up to run to him, but a wave of dizziness roils me. I tell my feet to run toward him, but they keep going in the opposite direction. Why can't I get them to go straight? The world spins as I fall to my knees again.

My clothes and my hair are soaked. My long, wet hair hangs in my eyes making it even harder to see. I reach for the sheriff as if sticking my hand out will somehow bring him closer.

He's not moving at all, so once again I struggle to my feet as I half stagger, half run to him, dropping to my knees next to his still form. There's a lot of blood coming from his head.

I watch it pool in the street just before the rain washes it away. His arm is in a weird position too. I grab for my phone, but it isn't in my pocket. Wait, the other pocket. It isn't there either. Where is my phone? It must have gone flying when Sheriff Mack pushed me out of the way.

"Help!" I scream. "Help me!" I don't know if anyone can hear me over the storm. Thankfully, several people from the night shift at the hotel appear in the entryway.

"Call an ambulance! Someone ran over Sheriff Mack!" Why was he here in the first place? Why didn't I take Wendy and Juliet up on their offer to watch over me? This is all my fault.

"Steve!" I sob. "Steve! Wake up! Please be okay! You have to be okay!" I slap his cheek like they do on tv because it's the only thing I can think of at the moment. I swear if he makes it out of this, the first thing I'll do is sign up for that dang first aid course I keep meaning to take.

"Steve!" I pat him on the cheek again as I hear sirens in the distance. I remember I have a blanket in the bus. He must be going into shock. I run to the bus, grabbing the keys that are still lying in the street. I fumble with the lock on the back door, everything is wet and slippery, and I still can't see, but finally get it open.

I quickly grab the colorful blanket, racing back to the sheriff, who still isn't moving. I place the blanket over him to try to keep him warm. I notice his mangled hat is lying in the middle of the street, and for some reason, I run over and grab it because I think it's important. I don't know why. Everything is moving in slow motion. What is taking that stupid ambulance so long?

"Please wake up! Please wake up!" I cry, my tears splashing onto his uniform mingle with the rain and his blood. He's getting paler by the moment. Then I hug him because I still can't think of what else I could be doing. I'm still squeezing him tight when the EMTs pull me off him.

"Ma'am, ma'am, let go. We've got it. Please, ma'am, let go." I finally release my grip as they pull me to my feet. They work on him immediately while another asks me if I'm okay. For some reason, he sounds like he's in a tunnel.

"Ma'am, you hit your head. Come with me."

"Am I bleeding?" I ask as I look down and see blood all over my clothes. I can't believe this. I'm bleeding to death right here. But how am I still standing?

"Ma'am, that's the sheriff's blood."

Oh. Yeah.

"You hit your head, but it doesn't seem too bad—hopefully just a scratch. You'll have a lump there tomorrow. Come with me, and I'll check you over."

"But Steve," I turn back to point at him.

"We're taking care of him. Let me check you out."

My knees are so wobbly and weak that the EMT puts his arm around me to prop me up. He helps me sit down on the back of an ambulance. Are there two ambulances, or am I imagining things?

I hear the other paramedics talking, and it's not good. Sheriff Mack has a nasty head injury and a dislocated shoulder. That explains the crooked arm.

They won't know about internal injuries until they get him to the hospital. I watch the ambulance speed away, sirens blaring, while I shiver uncontrollably. Someone gets a blanket and wraps it around me.

"I think you just bumped your head, and you have some scrapes here and there. You'll be sore tomorrow. But we'll take you to the hospital just to be safe."

"No, I'm good," I push him away. "I'm not in pain."

"Ma'am, it's the adrenaline talking. You should see a doctor. Besides, I can't let you drive."

"I can call someone," I tell him.

Then Deputy Owens appears in front of me. He's livid.

"Why do you keep showing up at crime scenes?" he snaps.

"Deputy, leave my patient alone. She's in no condition to be questioned."

I hold up my hand. I don't deserve defending. "I'm okay, thank you," I tell him. The paramedic gives up and steps back. I'm obviously not the best patient.

"What happened here?" the deputy snarls.

"I was trying to get into my car when some lunatic came from out of nowhere. He must have been drunk. The next thing I know, I'm on the ground. I think Sheriff Mack pushed me to safety but then got hit by the car. I don't know exactly what happened. It all went so fast. How is he? Will he be okay?"

I'm on the verge of tears right now, but I fear if I let them flow, they won't ever stop.

"We won't know for sure until the doctors check him out. It's bad."

I feel like throwing up. The sheriff just saved my life, and now he could die. All because of me.

"Can you tell me anything about who or what hit him? Car? Truck? SUV?" he barks at me.

"I think it was a car. A sedan. The lights were bright, and it all happened so fast." I press on my temples as if that will somehow make my brain work better and give me an answer.

"Yes, you mentioned that before. What color was the car?"

"I don't know. White? No blue. Wait, I think it was red."

The deputy shoots me a disgusted look, slamming his notebook shut. "I don't feel like dealing with all the paperwork that bringing you down to the station would entail, because I'm going to the hospital to check on the sheriff.

"But I promise you, I'll be on your doorstep bright and early tomorrow morning to question you further. I swear if you skip town, I will personally hunt you down and make you pay." His eyes bore into me before he stomps away.

Then he abruptly turns on his heel and marches back to me. This is it. He's changed his mind. He's arresting me and I'm going to jail, again. Instead, he snarls at me while snatching the sheriff's blood-spattered hat from my hands, then walks off again.

"He seems nice," the EMT mutters. I give him a weak smile. But I get it. He's worried about his friend and colleague, and he's right - he has discovered me at more crime scenes or accidents or whatever you want to call them lately than I care to admit.

When I hear Wendy and Juliet calling out to me, I swear I'm hallucinating. Maybe I hit my head harder than I thought. When they run to me, nearly knocking over the poor paramedic who must regret getting assigned to me by now, I know they're real.

"Are you okay?" Wendy sobs.

"What happened?" Juliet asks.

"You should have called us!" Wendy scolds me. "I knew something like this was going to happen. You know I had a bad feeling about this!"

"Don't worry about me. Worry about Steve!" I exclaim.

"Who?" Juliet asks.

"Uh, Sheriff Mack."

"Why? What happened to him?" Wendy asks, still looking over me for hidden injuries.

"He saved me! He pushed me out of the way. Some drunk almost ran me over!"

"Are you serious? Where is he now?" Juliet cries, with her hand covering her mouth in disbelief.

"The ambulance took him away. They don't know if he's going to make it!"

Then I sob. I never ask for help, even when I have friends who are happy to give it to me. This is all my fault.

29

D eputy Owens is on my doorstep the following morning, demanding answers. Sheriff Mack's surgery went well, thank goodness, but it's still touch and go. The next 24 hours are crucial for him. He dislocated his shoulder, cracked two ribs, and sustained a concussion.

The concussion is the most worrisome. He isn't conscious yet, so they haven't been able to question him. I'm desperate to ask the deputy to keep me updated, but I'm sure he'll shut me down and refuse. He blames me for his boss's condition. He has every right to.

Why didn't I listen to Wendy's premonition? They offered to keep an eye on me. Why didn't I take them up on it? It's still hard for me to imagine having friends I can rely on. Now I realize that has to change. I have to let people in.

The deputy is disappointed I don't have any more answers than I did last night. So far, all they know is the sheriff was across the street investigating a break-in. They think he must have seen me and the car, then pushed me out of the way.

Even Mystery and Clara know how serious this is. Neither said a word while the deputy was at the house. Mystery didn't even shout popo. I don't know if that impresses me or scares me.

Wendy and Juliet brought me home last night. I vaguely re-member changing into some dry pajamas while Wendy made a special tea to help me relax and heal. I heard them explain to

Clara what had happened, knowing that she would be worried and listening in, even though they couldn't see her, which I thought was nice of them.

"What next?" Clara asks after the deputy leaves.

"I'm going for a drive to clear my head," I tell her. "The bus is in the garage so one of the ladies obviously drove it home for me."

"It was Wendy," she responds, nodding in agreement. "Are you sure you're okay to drive?"

"Yes, I'm fine, thank you. I won't be gone long."

Neither one dares to ask if they can come along. That's how dire the situation is. Before even I realize what I'm doing, I drive up Red Mountain again. After I swore I'd never return. It had nothing to do with Pavel. He is delightful company.

It's just that the incident with the broken-down bus scared me. I don't even care about that anymore. Let the bus break down 100 times. I just need Sheriff Mack to pull through. Remy as well.

In case you're wondering, yes, I remembered to stop at the store on the way to get pork rinds. I'm not *that* far out of it.

"I thought I might be seeing you today," Pavel says when I appear on his doorstep.

"It's been a brutal week," I tell him.

"Lay it on me, dove!" he responds, gesturing to the floor.

We sit down and I explain everything that happened since we last talked. "Sheriff Mack wouldn't be lying in a hospital bed right now if I had accepted my friends' offer for help. If I had only listened to them when they warned me to be careful. I seriously screwed up."

"Do you remember what I told you last time you were here?"

I hang my head in shame. "I do, but I obviously didn't listen to you."

"Yet my advice still stands," he tells me in a soft voice.

"What do you mean? It's too late!" I cry.

"It's never too late for you to do better," he reminds me. "Of course, you can't change what has already happened, but you can change what *will* happen. *Now* you can do differently, and you never have to be alone again. You only have to trust those who have already *proven* they can be trusted. I think your new friends have more than done that."

I nod, a tear sliding down my cheek. "You're right," I whisper.

"Have they identified the car that almost hit you?" he asks.

"No! Just one more thing I screwed up last night. I saw the car leave. I know I looked right at the license plate, but with everything that happened, I can't remember."

"Have you ever been hypnotized?" Pavel asks.

"What? No!" I recoil in fear. What is he suggesting?

"It's nothing to fear. We don't have to do it. I just thought I'd suggest it as a means of gently accessing your subconscious. You're sure you saw the car after it hit Sheriff Mack?"

"Yes," I nod my head emphatically. "I remember looking right at it as it sped away. I couldn't process what had happened at the time. I was trying to figure out how I ended up on the ground without being hit by the car. I know it was a sedan and I think it was white, or blue, or red. But that's all I know. Does that sound stupid?"

"Not at all, dove. You'd just been through a highly traumatic event. Your mind was awhirl and could only consciously process a minimum of facts. But I assure you, the rest of your brain stored the details. We just need to access that."

"If I let you hypnotize me, you promise you won't make me cluck like a chicken?" I demand.

"Why does everyone think that's what happens when they get hypnotized?" he asks.

"I don't know," I shrug. "It's the first thing that popped into my head."

"Hypnosis allows us to access the part of your brain that stores all the information surrounding what happened last night, bringing it to the surface. I can only access what you allow me to see. I won't be asking you to reveal your deepest, darkest secrets. In case you were worried about that," he adds.

"Oh, I wasn't," I tell him. Okay, I was. "All right. I'll do anything to catch the person who did this. Let's hypnotize me."

"Groovy!" Pavel cries. "Now get comfortable. I need you to relax completely. That's it. Close your eyes and concentrate on the sound of my voice. I'll count down from three…"

Just as I'm about to tell him I know this will never work on me, I hear him counting three, two, one.

"You can open your eyes now," he says.

"It didn't work," I slump in disappointment. "Wait! It was a sedan. It was white! I see the license plate! Quick! Get me something to write on!"

He grins at me, holding up a piece of paper with a license plate number. "What do you mean, it didn't work?"

"But I felt nothing!" I insist.

"You were under for nearly ten minutes. You relayed every-thing that happened last night after the car hit the sheriff."

"But I don't feel any different. Except it's all much clearer now! I know who almost ran me down and hit Sheriff Mack. I mean, I don't know who exactly, but I know the car. Pavel, thank you so much, but I have to go. I have to get the license plate to the deputy."

"Good luck, my dear," he says, bowing at me again, but this time I bow back. I guess I still prefer shaking hands if you want the truth. "Holly, one more thing. Don't be too hard on yourself for failing to reach out to your friends. After all, you overcame your fears and traveled all the way up here for help, didn't you?"

30

I'm on my way to the Sheriff's Department with the license plate number when my phone rings.

"Ms. Daniel? This is Nurse Marissa calling from Glenwood Springs Memorial Hospital."

Oh no, this is it. Either Remy or Sheriff Mack took a turn for the worse. Or one of them died. Or both! I don't think I can handle this. My heart races a million miles an hour. I can't breathe. This is the worst.

"Yes?" I squeak.

"We have a Remy Cashmore here."

"Yes," I gulp, trying to steady myself.

"Ms. Cashmore is awake. She asked me to call you. Can you get to the hospital as soon as possible?"

I make a hasty u-turn in the middle of the road infuriating several drivers in the process. While I race to the hospital, I feel a little sheepish. I'm not sure why I thought they'd be calling *me* with news about Sheriff Mack. Fortunately, I didn't blurt out anything inappropriate.

Why would Remy want to see me, though? Whatever the reason, I hope she has the answers I need.

I find the closest parking spot I can, leap from the bus and run into the lobby. I pause to catch my breath while pressing the elevator button repeatedly, but that takes too long so I sprint for the stairwell instead.

I run down the hallway to Remy's room, ignoring the nurse yelling at me that there's no running in the hospital. I don't care.

I was so worried that Remy wouldn't make it, I never thought about what I would do if she survived. Except ask who did this to her!

I pause in the doorway of her room. She's pale and fragile looking. Her black marker eyebrows are gone. She looks a lot better without them.

Her eyes are closed. Should say something or just wait a bit? I quietly clear my throat and they flutter open. She smiles when she sees me. What a relief!

"Hey there Remy, how are you feeling?"

"I'm tired and I have a headache, but not bad otherwise," she whispers.

"Have the police been by yet?"

"No, not yet."

"I have to ask, what happened? Did someone do this to you?" I don't want to appear indelicate, but I really need to know what's going on and I need to know now.

She gestures at me to come closer. "I stole the doll!" she whispers.

Oh, dear. It's just as I suspected. "I'm sure you didn't mean to kill Mr. Beasley. It was an accident, right?"

"Oh! No! You misunderstand. I didn't kill him. He was dead when I got there. Then I saw you coming, so I panicked. I grabbed the doll and ran! I swear I didn't even go there to steal it. I just wanted to see it up close before the crowds showed up.

"When I saw him lying under the bookcase, I don't know what came over me. I just knew I had to have that doll. Then I ran to a payphone at the end of the street and called the cops."

"You're the reason I heard the back door shut?"

"Yes! That was me!"

"Did you have the doll in the lockbox in that room in your house?" If I thought my heart was racing before, it's nothing compared to what it's doing now.

She nods her head slowly. "You were in there looking for it, weren't you?"

Oops. "Yes, I was," I admit reluctantly. If we're confessing to things, I might as well say it.

"They tell me you found me and called the ambulance."

"I found out that you lied about your alibi for the night Mr. Beasley was killed." She nods her head glumly. "So, I came back to talk to you about it."

"That's when you found me. What about the doll? Did you check when you were there?"

"I did. The lockbox was open, and the doll was gone."

"Oh no! I knew that would happen!" she cries. "I'm a horrible person. Do you know that I even lost one of her shoes while I was running away? I shouldn't be allowed to have dolls!" she continues to wail.

Yes, I did know that, but that's for another discussion.

"Remy, I have to ask, did you swallow the poison on purpose?"

"You don't know?"

"Know what?" I ask.

"I didn't swallow it on purpose," she murmurs.

I beg silently. *Please don't tell me it was the doll.* I do *not* know what to do with a possessed doll.

"It was Dustin Holmes."

31

I try to check on Sheriff Mack after I leave Remy's room, but the front desk refuses to tell me which room he's in. I notice there is a large police presence in the hospital. It scares me to think they're worried that whoever did this might come after him again if he can identify them.

Next, I drive straight to the Sheriff's Department. They'll want to find out who this license plate belongs to. Plus I want them them to research a public record for me.

The clerk summons the deputy for me while I wait at the front desk. He isn't happy to see me. I'm not his favorite person right now.

"Come to confess?" he asks.

"Confess what?"

"Anything? Everything?" he grunts, his arms crossed over his chest in a defiant stance.

"I have the license plate number and description of the car that hit the sheriff last night." I explain, holding the piece of paper up in front of him.

"Come with me," he insists, so I wordlessly follow him down the hallway and into an office. "Where did you get this?"

I didn't think he'd ask me that. Should I tell him I was hypnotized? Somehow I don't think he'd be thrilled about that.

"After some deep soul searching it came to me," I explain. It's not a lie after all.

"I don't want to know, do I?"

I shake my head. "Probably not."

He enters the license plate number into the system. "Well, what do you know?" he says.

"What? Who is it?" I ask.

Deputy Owens stares back at me like he has no intention of letting me know what he discovered.

"Oh, come on! I got the number for you. Please tell me who it is!" I beg.

"What kind of car did you say it was?"

"A big white sedan. I don't know what kind though." I raise my hands in ignorance. I don't know cars. I just know my pink bus.

"The car is registered to Dustin Holmes."

32

—— • ——

"**D**ustin Holmes?" I shriek. "Are you kidding me? Dustin Holmes?" I yell so loud another deputy comes to check on us.

"Everything is fine here," Deputy Owens waves him off.

"He poisoned Remy Cashmore!"

"He what?" Now it's Deputy Owens turn to shout. "How do you know that?"

"I was just at the hospital. She told me."

"Why did she tell *you*? *We* haven't even spoken to her yet." Now he's grumpy again.

"I don't know, she had the nurse call me. I just assumed you guys were on your way."

He shakes his head, snatching the phone out of the cradle, fiercely jabbing at the numbers so hard I'm convinced he'll break it. "Get over to Remy Cashmore's room right now. She's awake and talking." He slams the phone down, glaring at me. "You can go now. Thank you for your help."

"Hold on a second. Could I ask just one teeny tiny favor?" I can't believe I have the guts to ask him this right now. I won't be surprised if he throws me out, but I have to know.

"What is it?" he sighs.

I hold out a second piece of paper to him. "Is there a way for you to check this person's birth certificate?"

"That would be in the records department. Next building over."

"Okay, thank you," I tell him.

Then he groans like he can't believe he's doing this either. "You can tell him them I sent you."

"Thank you! I appreciate it!" I squeal running out the door.

33

Wendy and Juliet are meeting me at my house so I can read everyone in on my plan. I admit, my first thought was to go at this alone, but then I remind myself Sheriff Mack wouldn't be in the hospital right now if I had asked for help to begin with.

I didn't even have to ask for it. Wendy and Juliet offered. Scratch that, they insisted. I have friends I trust now, and I won't forget that.

I was surprised when Deputy Owens agrees to the meeting as well. They've searched high and low for Dustin but can't find him.

The four of us gather at my kitchen table with fresh coffee and pastries from Juliet's bakery. Oops, make that five. Clara is here too, of course.

"What's the deal with the empty chair?" Deputy Owens asks, pointing at it.

Wendy, Juliet, Clara, and I answer in unison. "It's not empty."

Of course, only I can hear Clara. All right, Mystery too, as she points out from the countertop where she's perched.

"Seriously?" he asks. "There's a ghost here? The sheriff told me about this. Can she see me?"

Clara glares at him. She's still mad that it's the deputy instead of Sheriff Mack. I reminded her we should just be grateful that the sheriff is even alive.

"Yes, she can see you. She can hear you too."

The deputy looks increasingly uncomfortable. He's out of his element here. Surrounded by a bunch of ladies and two ghosts. I guess I'd be uncomfortable too if I didn't know any better.

"Deputy Owens already knows most of this, but I haven't had the chance to update you ladies yet," I explain.

Wendy and Juliet lean forward, eager to hear the news.

"In a nutshell, Remy Cashmore stole the Bebe Mothereau after accidentally stumbling across Mr. Beasley's body, then Dustin Holmes tried to kill Remy, then stole the doll for himself because he's broke."

Wendy is so shocked, all she can do is make noises that sound kind of like jumbled words.

Juliet just sits there with her mouth hanging open.

"Oh, and Dustin also tried to run me down – we assume to get the doll's shoe - but hit Sheriff Mack instead."

Juliet's head swivels from me to Deputy Owens and back again.

The deputy is so mad at hearing this again, he clenches his fists hard enough I'm worried he'll break something.

Juliet pushes the plate of pastries closer to him as a peace offering.

"Do you have any of those colorful cookie sandwiches?" he asks. "The sheriff was telling me about those."

Juliet checks the box and I'm relieved when she pulls some out. I wasn't sure what would happen if she didn't have any. Deputy Owens visibly relaxes after eating one. Cookies are so soothing.

"Remy told me that without the shoe, the doll is worth far less. Therefore, I'm going to draw Dustin out by offering to sell him the shoe."

"I don't see how you think you can get him to talk to you when the trained professionals at the Sheriff's Department can't find him. I'm sure he's left the state by now. If not the country," the deputy insists.

"I think if he was desperate enough to run me down to get it, he'll take the deal I'm offering him," I point out.

"Deal?" Wendy asks.

She and Juliet are still shocked over everything I just revealed. They almost don't know what to say.

"I'll text Dustin to tell him I still have the shoe, but I'm willing to sell it to him. I'll suggest we meet somewhere - like the museum to make the exchange. Deputy Owens will go early to hide in the museum. Once he hands me the money, Owens will take him into custody," I explain pointing at the deputy.

"We should hide in the museum too!" Wendy says.

"No!" Deputy Owens responds so sharply we all jump.

"You two will hide across the street as backup," I offer.

I can tell the deputy doesn't like it, but at least it's better than civilians hiding in the museum. He'll just have to accept it because they're my friends and they're witches and I want them nearby.

"What about me?" Clara asks.

"And me!" Mystery adds.

"You will be in the bus."

"Last time we got to chase down the bad guys!" Clara exclaims. "That was a hoot! Do you remember?"

"Yes, I remember, and I don't plan to chase after any bad guys again," I respond emphatically.

"What?" I ask. When I see Wendy and Juliet cringe.

"Don't jinx yourself!" Juliet says.

"I'm not worried." I roll my eyes at their jinx talk.

Then Deputy Owens cringes.

"You too?" I exclaim.

"I'm with these ladies. Jinxes are real. Hey, can I have another cookie?"

Juliet pushes the plate directly in front of him.

"I love these creme filled macaroons."

"They're macrons," Juliet says using the correct pronunciation.

"That's what I said!" he insists.

She doesn't bother to correct him again.

"Oh, I almost forgot," Deputy Owens says.

We wait with bated breath thinking this must be important.

"We found Abby from the pool, and she confirmed your alibi for Monday night."

I don't quite know how to respond to this, so I ignore him. Considering I never should have been a person of interest *or* a suspect in the first place.

"So, we're all in agreement?" Everyone nods their heads. "Then I'll text Dustin and put the plan in motion."

"Are you sure he'll be willing to meet in the museum? What if he says no?" the deputy asks.

"He's so focused on getting this shoe and selling the doll, I don't think he'll question it."

"I hope you're right," he claims. "But don't be surprised when he says no."

"Here goes nothing." I push send on the text.

Me: I have the shoe. $5,000 cash.

It takes all of 30 minutes for Dustin to write back.

Dustin: Where/When can we meet?

Me: The doll museum. Midnight.

Dustin: Fine. But come alone! Any funny business and you're dead.

34

Deputy Owens insists that he and Wendy and Juliet get into position at 10 PM as a precaution. Dustin may notice the commotion if they cut it too close to midnight. We don't think he'll go too early though, because he still has to stay in hiding.

Shortly before midnight, I double check the shoe is in my pocket, while Clara, Mystery, and I head to the museum. I hate to admit it, but Clara is right. This all seems eerily familiar.

Mystery was mad when Clara got home last time and told her what a great time she had chasing after bad guys and watching the 'chick fight' as she called it.

Mystery then insisted we include her in any future expeditions, just in case. I hope none of us has to experience too much excitement this time. I don't care what the others say about jinxes either.

I pull into the empty parking lot at 11:59 PM with my pulse racing like a snare drum. Forget butterflies in my stomach. I have eagles flapping around in there.

I nervously walk into the museum through the unlocked front door as Deputy Owens suggested. If Dustin is watching, to make sure I'm alone, he'll see he can do the same. Just like we predicted, less than two minutes later, he walks in the front door as well.

He sneers at me. "Where's the shoe?"

"Where's the money?" I ask.

"You'll get your money when I get my shoe," he says.

"You need to show me the money first. How do I know you even have \$5,000 on you?" Deputy Owens coached me on this. He said I must insist that Dustin show me the money. When he proves he came with cash, then they can arrest him.

"Are you implying that I'm broke?" he snaps.

"Oh, I *know* you're broke. Show me the money. Now!" I may sound tough, but my knees are knocking together I'm so scared. I'm surprised that my voice sounds at least somewhat normal; I expected it to come out with a squeak.

"Women," he grumbles as he reaches into his pocket, pulling out a wad of cash. The amount isn't actually important the deputy said. He just has to prove he came with money to buy the shoe.

But just as I anticipate Deputy Owens jumping out to tell Dustin he's under arrest, Bianca appears.

35

"Leave my friend alone!" she shouts, attempting to knock a bookcase over onto Deputy Owens. Thankfully, it isn't nearly as big as the one that killed Mr. Beasley. He dives out of the way but it clips him across the shoulder.

"Bianca!" I gasp. "Don't!"

"This man was hiding from you, Holly!" she exclaims.

"No, you don't under--"

It's enough of a distraction that the deputy staggers several steps allowing Dustin to wrap his arm around my neck, pulling me against him. I nearly panic when he pulls out a gun, brandishing it at the deputy.

"I said no funny business!" he shouts. "I knew this would happen!" He strengthens his grip on my neck so hard I can barely breathe. If he squeezes any tighter, I'll pass out.

Bianca moves toward us. "No Bianca, don't!" I shout. "Please back off!"

Since I'm the only one who can see her, I don't want Dustin to get spooked and start firing his gun indiscriminately. He could hit Deputy Owens!

"Who are you talking to?" Dustin sneers. "Who's Bianca?"

"Just go, okay? The deputy will let you go. I'm sure of it. Just don't shoot anybody," I beg.

"I'm going, but you're coming with me. You're my ticket out of here!"

Dustin drags me out of the museum, while Bianca follows us. His arm is still wrapped firmly around my neck but at least now I can breathe.

"Which car is yours?" he asks when we get outside.

"It's the only other car here," I point at the bus.

"Don't get smart with me, missy!" he growls, tightening his grip.

Why do I have such a big mouth?

"Get in!" he demands, still waving the gun in my face.

While I climb up into the driver's seat I seriously consider taking off. If I knew I could run over him like he did Sheriff Mack, I'd do it. But I'm worried I'll miss and he'll shoot me.

The deputy is still inside but what if Dustin shoots him or Wendy or Juliet across the street? I can't risk it.

"What's going on?" Clara cries. "Who is this?" she asks as Bianca joins us in the VW.

"We screwed up," I tell her. Dustin then climbs into the passenger seat, forcing Clara to dive into the back with Bianca and Mystery.

"*We* screwed up?" Mystery asks.

"Bianca screwed up," I hiss, jabbing my thumb in her direction.

"The cat talks?" Bianca says.

"Who are *you*?" Mystery asks.

"You're the spirit I saw in the front yard during the rainstorm!" Clara exclaims.

"Just drive and quit flapping your jaws!" Dustin barks pointing the gun at me again.

Then he looks in the backseat. "Who are you talking to, anyway? Hey, you better not be wearing a wire." He tugs at my shirt to check.

"Touch me again and I don't care how many guns you have, you'll regret it. You definitely won't get your shoe back," I tell him, slapping his hand away.

Between now and when he dragged me from the museum, I decided it would be best to pretend I don't have the shoe on me. I hope it will buy me some time.

36

"I left the shoe at home, in a safe place," I tell Dustin.

"What are you talking about? The shoe is in your pocket. I saw you," Clara reminds me.

"What do you mean you left it at home?" Dustin snarls.

"You saw the deputy back there. It was obviously a trap. When you showed me the money, they were going to arrest you. Why would I bring the shoe only to risk you somehow grabbing it and running?"

"She's playing him, you dummy," Mystery explains to Clara. "She's stalling for time."

"Oh, I got it. Don't call me dummy, dummy."

Just what I always wanted. To be kidnapped by a murderous psychopath while listening to squabbling spirits in the back seat.

"Holly, can you believe this?" Clara says. "It's just like last time, except we aren't chasing the bad guys; the bad guy is in the car with us!"

"Yes, isn't this fun!" I tell her.

"I don't know who you're talking to, you weirdo, but it's creeping me out," Dustin says.

I consider telling him I'm talking to the voices in my head, but the truth is much more dramatic, and I want to keep him off his game. "There are three ghosts in the back seat of this bus."

Dustin whirls around to check as if by saying that, he'll suddenly be able to see the ghosts himself.

"I don't see anything," he announces.

"You can't see them. I'm a spirit communicator. That's how I can talk to them."

He narrows his eyes at me. He obviously doesn't believe that and thinks I'm unbalanced, which is good. I don't want him to think he has kidnapped a stable person who will do whatever he wants.

I want him to consider me unpredictable. I just hope the Sheriff's Department checks at home for us because, beyond acting unhinged, I don't have any other plans.

"Did you tell Bianca you know she killed her dad?" Clara asks.

Bianca gasps.

While we're looking to kill time, we might as well get this out of the way.

"No, I didn't tell her that I know Mr. Beasley is her father, or that she killed him, Clara, but thanks for helping with that."

"Well, how was I supposed to know?" Clara snaps.

"How did you find out?" Bianca asks.

"I looked up your birth certificate in the county records," I explain. "It lists Mr. Beasley as your dad. After Clara saw you in our front yard that night, and I glimpsed you on the street corner, I knew something was amiss. I realized you must be a poltergeist, so I wondered what else you were lying about. I took a chance and looked up your birth certificate."

Bianca remains in the back seat, her mouth hanging open but speechless.

"Well, if you're so smart, do you know I'm the one who loosened the bolt on your alternator so you'd get stuck in the middle of nowhere?" she throws back at me.

Whoa. How did I miss that? "I didn't realize that," I respond slowly.

"Hang on a second, hang on a second," Dustin interrupts. "Who killed Beasley? I thought it was the crazy doll collector chick. With the weird eyebrows."

"The one *you* tried to kill?" I remind him.

"Yeah, her!" he exclaims.

I sigh. Just when I think things can't get any weirder.

"Mr. Beasley's daughter is a poltergeist. Poltergeists, unlike traditional spirits, can move things. Bianca pushed the oak bookcase over on her father, who she hated for abandoning her and her mother, and crushed him."

"Seriously?" Dustin responds.

"Seriously."

"It's not like I believe you or anything!" he retorts. "This is ridiculous!"

"I don't care if you believe me or not. It's true," I explain.

He slides his hand down his face. "How did I get myself into this situation?"

"I keep asking myself that same question," I tell him.

37

—·—

When I pull into the driveway at my house, everything appears quiet. If the cops are here, they're hiding.

Deputy Owens knows where I live, but I'm not sure he'd realize that I'm just wacky enough to bring a killer to my own home. Sheriff Mack, on the other hand. He'd *definitely* know I'm wacky enough to bring a killer here. Of course, I'd never hear the end of it.

"Get out," Dustin tells me. "Take me to the shoe."

"Then you'll go on your way?" I ask him. "I'll even let you have my bus."

Clara gasps in surprise. It's not like I *want* to give him the bus, but I doubt he's willing to call a ride share service. Wouldn't the driver have a story to tell on that one?

"Just get me the shoe," he says.

"You guys wait here!" I tell the spirits. I'm not sure why I insist on that, except I don't need them tagging along behind us, asking questions, adding sarcastic commentary.

"The shoe is in the garage," I tell him, pointing at it.

Before leaving I pause for a moment to stare at Bianca. For some weird reason I want to say she looks pale. Or paler. She's a ghost after all. I wonder if poltergeists can alter their looks. Something else I'll have to ask Pavel someday. If I make it that long.

"Stop stalling and go!" Dustin says, jerking the gun in my direction.

I trudge toward the garage. Where are the cops? After I open the door, I quickly glance around, trying to figure out how to get the shoe out of my pocket and into a hiding spot. It would be great if I could find a weapon, but I just cleaned last week, and unfortunately, everything is all tucked away, neat and tidy.

That's what I get for trying to be more organized. I stare longingly at a shovel hanging from the wall on a hook I installed. It would be too obvious if I tried to get it down, and I'm not quick enough. When he sees me staring at the shovel, Dustin shoves me. "Don't even think about it," he says.

"It's in the refrigerator," I tell him.

"You put the shoe in the garage refrigerator?" he asks.

"Would you have thought of that?" I retort.

"No, I guess not. But I'll open the fridge," he insists, pushing me aside. "I don't want you pulling a weapon out of there."

Rats. I didn't think of that.

"Yes! Good idea!" I exclaim. "*You* open the fridge."

He eyes me suspiciously. "On second thought, what if you booby-trapped it knowing that I'd insist on opening it myself?"

"No, I'd never do that!" I plead. Thank goodness criminals are dumb.

"Now I *really* don't believe you! Open the fridge. But don't try anything!"

He pushes me forward, carefully eyeing the refrigerator door the entire time, giving me just enough space to slide the shoe out of my pocket and tuck it in my hand. When I open the door, he backs up several steps like it might explode.

"I put it in the crisper drawer," I tell him, opening the drawer and magically producing the shoe. For one awful moment, I realize he'll expect the shoe to be cold.

Yet when I hand it to him, he snatches it from me, looks at it, then stuffs it into his own pocket. He clearly doesn't realize the shoe isn't refrigerated. Phew. Did I mention how dumb criminals are?

"Will you leave now, at least? Here, you can take my car," I tell him, dangling the keys in front of him.

"Are you kidding me? If I leave here alone in that bright pink monstrosity of yours, I won't get more than a block before the cops pounce. You're still my ticket out of here and to the airport. You and your 'ghosts,'" he says laughingly, making air quotes around the word ghosts. "Let's go." He gestures at the door.

"Fine," I grumble, leading us back to the bus.

"Hey, what's going on?" Mystery says when we return.

"Where are we going now?" Clara asks.

"We're taking Mr. Holmes here to the airport," I explain.

"The minute I get on an airplane, all of you," he says, waving his hand toward the backseat, "can be on your way. Do you think they heard me?" he laughs.

"They heard you," I sigh.

"What a jerk!" Mystery exclaims.

"You think?" I ask.

I carefully merge onto I-70 as we head toward Glenwood Canyon and the airport.

38

"Since you plan to get on a plane and disappear after this, do you mind if I ask you some questions?"

"Sure, why not?" Dustin responds.

"Oh! Ask him about the file cabinet!" Bianca chimes in from the back seat. "Did it hurt?"

"File cabinet?" I ask.

"Yes!" Bianca insists.

"Bianca wants to know if the file cabinet hurt."

Dustin pivots in his seat. "How did you know... oh, wait, I told you about that the other day. When I followed you to the food truck and realized you had the shoe."

"You followed me there?" I exclaim in shock.

"Well, yeah, you were acting really weird. I wasn't sure how much you knew about me, so I decided to follow you for a while. Plus, I saw you at Remy's the first time I was there, which made me suspicious of your motives."

"Ha! I told you I saw someone sneaking around at Remy's!" Clara exclaims.

"That woman who almost knocked me down..." I snap my fingers.

"Oh, I had nothing to do with that," he says. "That was just a happy coincidence."

"I see."

"But that was when I realized you had the shoe, of course," he reminds me.

"So, you thought you'd run me down to get it!"

"Yeah, and that stupid sheriff had to intervene. There you were, just standing in the middle of the street, staring into the headlights with your mouth hanging open, totally paralyzed. I was sure it would be so easy. Then, out of nowhere, the sheriff rockets across the street, flinging you out of the way. I was so mad!"

"I want to know if the file cabinet hurt!" Bianca demands, kicking the back of my seat.

"Don't kick my seat!" I yell back while Dustin gawks at me like I'm the weirdest person he's ever met. Yeah, I'm the weird one here.

"Did it hurt when you got hit by the file cabinet?"

"Yes, it hurt like the dickens. I needed six stitches," he says.

"Good!" Bianca responds smugly.

"Did you hit him with the file cabinet drawer?" I ask her.

"Yes! For not paying his child support."

"Oh!" I exclaim. It's hard not to laugh at that. "Bianca says she hit you with the file cabinet because you didn't pay your child support."

He glances in the back seat to make sure he still can't see the spirits.

"Bianca, put that finger down!" I tell her. It's like a circus in here. I check her out in the rearview mirror again. She's faded even more since we left my house. "Clara, is it just me..."

"Nope! I see it too. She's fading fast."

"Do you know why?" I ask.

"No clue."

Then, just as I think everything is going about as smoothly as it can, given the circumstances, the bus sputters and dies.

What the heck? "Not again! Of all the stupid times to break down on me!" I shout, maneuvering the bus over to the side of the road.

"Heyyyy, what are you trying to pull?" Dustin bellows.

"I'm not trying to pull anything! It's an old car. Sometimes it breaks down, you know!"

"It can't break down now! I have to get to the airport! Can't you make it go?"

"Do I look like a mechanic?" I snap.

"My cousin works at Joe's. You should take it there," he insists.

"I was just there!" I yell back. Am I seriously arguing with a gun-wielding maniac? Is this what my life has become?

"You wait here. I'll pull someone over," he tells me, jumping out of the bus.

"Great, you do that."

I watch Dustin stand at the side of the road with his thumb out like he's hitchhiking, while waving the gun around with his other hand. I don't think people believe it's a real gun. Some flip him off. Others shake their fists. Still, others swerve around him and speed up.

If I could get the stupid bus to go, I could peel out and leave him standing at the side of the road. I try starting it again, but nothing happens. It's like last time. If only I knew what Sheriff Mack did to fix it with that pen.

Then I see it. In the rearview mirror. That can't be what I think it is, can it? It's a black SUV from the Sheriff's Department. Yes! Thank goodness for Deputy Owens.

I jump out of the VW just in time to watch Dustin drop his gun, throwing his hands in the air while Sheriff Mack approaches. I mean Deputy Owens. No, I mean Sheriff Mack, with his arm in a sling and bandage on his head. How did he get here?

He tosses his handcuffs to me. I'm so impressed with myself when I actually catch them.

"Don't just stand there gawking. Cuff him!" he orders. Oh wow. I can't believe I get to handcuff a perp. I can say perp, right? This is the best day ever. I handcuff Dustin, who is thoroughly confused at this point. He's not the only one.

I laugh out loud when I hear Clara cheering in the VW.

"I thought I told you to get that thing fixed," Sheriff Mack says, nodding his head at the bus.

"I did!" I tell him. "Joe replaced the bolt, and triple-checked it. He told me there was no way it was coming out on its own again..."

Then I turn back to the VW to see a very faded Bianca put her hands in the air and shrug.

"How did you find me?" I ask. I'm so stunned I almost don't know what to say.

"You're welcome?" he offers.

"Of course, thank you very much." Now I'm embarrassed. That should have been the first thing out of my mouth. I still want to know how he managed this.

Shouldn't he be in the hospital? "Now that I've thanked you, will you tell me how you found me?"

"I was at home where I was supposed to be resting when I heard what was happening over the police scanner. I knew the first thing you'd do was something crazy like driving him to your house hoping that we'd be hiding there, waiting to apprehend him," he starts.

Ha! I knew he'd know that!

"But it took me a while to get myself together," he gestures to the sling. "By the time I got there, you'd already gone. So I contacted a buddy who works for the company that maintains the live feed cameras in Glenwood Canyon. We spotted that pink beast right away." He chuckles at his own cleverness.

Imagine if I had painted it beige like I'd threatened to do in the beginning? They may not have found us.

"I also assumed you were going to the airport, but I was concerned you had too much of a head start. I alerted the authorities at the Eagle County Airport to intercept you. But lo-and-behold, here you are at the side of the road once again."

"I'm incredibly grateful," I tell him.

"I'd take some more of those cookie sandwiches," he says.

What is the deal with those macarons?

"I will ensure you get a lifetime supply!" I tell him.

"Cool! Hey, do you have another pen?"

As I search the bus for another pen, Sheriff Mack watches Dustin, and several more SUVs from the department arrive to assist us. The deputies question the Sheriff and me about what happened.

We're all shocked when Dustin suddenly bolts toward the trees lining the side of the road.

In a flash, a barely visible Bianca flies out of the bus, chases Dustin, then trips him. The handcuffs, make it impossible to keep his balance. He falls right on his face, flopping about like a fish out of water. The sheriff's deputies descend on him, scoop him up, and haul him back to their vehicles. Where did he think was going?

Bianca, who is nearly invisible now, even to me, waves at me. I wave back, and poof, she's gone. I cry out in shock as I whirl around to see if Clara noticed.

Clara, hangs out the bus window, shouting, "Where did she go?"

Even Mystery looks surprised.

I don't know what just happened. Is she gone for good? She didn't just disappear like I see spirits do all the time. It's more like she just ceased to exist.

39

The re-grand opening for the Glenwood Doll Museum is in full swing. The entire town must be here! The judge sentenced Remy to about a billion hours of community service, so they agreed to let her manage the museum as a full-time volunteer.

In his will, Mr. Beasley left the museum to the town, so the city council agreed to a one-year trial for Remy as manager. Assuming she does a good job, and the museum is self-supporting, they'll allow her to continue.

Surprise, surprise, we negotiated a truce with the poltergeists. Remy agreed to a Poltergeist Friday where they get to act out and put on a show - they aren't allowed to break things or hurt anyone - but they're encouraged to entertain visitors and tourists by doing spooky things. Now that the negative energy that surrounded Bianca is gone, they're much less destructive.

Tourists are so eager to experience the haunted museum they've booked tickets weeks in advance. They say it's the most visitors they've ever had.

Sheriff Mack is here in a tie and sport coat. He's talking and laughing with some of his colleagues and looks so different that I walk right past him without recognizing him.

"Ms. Daniel!" he bellows.

"Sheriff Mack!" I exclaim. "You look different!"

He crooks his head at me. "Different good or different bad?"

"I think different good."

"Really?" he stands a little taller.

"Yes, really. The bruises on your face are healing nicely as well." He sustained several gashes on his face after being run down by Dustin, but it looks like they're healing quickly. His arm is still in a sling which I'm sure he hates.

"By the way in case I haven't thanked you for saving my life twice. Thank you."

"You're welcome. Again." He nods curtly but then seems embarrassed, so he wanders off in search of some more punch. But not before pausing and looking back at me. "Don't think I didn't hear you call me Steve, by the way."

"Excuse me?"

"After I saved your life and got run over by a madman. You said *Steve don't die*."

"Oh. That."

I want to throw something at him when he smirks and walks away. I wonder if I could do it and blame it on a poltergeist.

"Pavel!" I exclaim with surprise when he appears in front of me.

"I couldn't miss the museum's new opening," he says. "I'm also certain you have questions for me."

"I sure do!" I hug him in greeting.

Without asking, he knows exactly what I'm thinking. "Bianca's lifelong hatred of her father and her need to keep it a secret fueled her existence. Once you uncovered the secret and then told her, it lost its power."

"That's why she started fading right after I told her."

"That can happen," he nods knowingly.

"But at the very end, when she finally just disappeared, why did that happen?"

"It must have taken a great deal of energy to help you," he explains.

"Which wasn't negative energy," I add.

"Precisely."

"Is it okay that I was a little sad to see her go, even after all the trouble she caused? I get that she killed someone, after all."

"You had many things in common with her. I can see why you liked the good parts of her."

"She really couldn't stick around, could she? For everyone's sake." I lament.

"No," he says. We stand in silence for a moment, reflecting on everything that happened. "Hey, did someone say they have champagne here?"

"They do," I laugh. "The table over there."

"Then I'll get some. Don't be a stranger, dig it?"

"I'll see you soon, I'm sure!"

He flashes me a peace sign, and off he goes.

"Pardon me, aren't you the ghost whisperer everyone is talking about?" a tall, thin woman with almond-shaped eyes asks me. I don't recognize her. I've noticed that in a small town, I'm beginning to recognize a lot of people in the grocery store, at the brewery, and now at the museum, of course. But I've never seen this woman before.

"I'm a paranormal private investigator, to be exact. Is there something I can help you with?"

"The Precious Peridot was stolen."

"Someone stole your jewelry?" I'm confused. Why would she need me? Unless she thinks a spirit, or a poltergeist stole it. After this week's crisis, I think I'm done with poltergeists for a while.

Perhaps this will be another case of someone's cat hiding their jewelry. I'm down for a simple case right now.

She looks at me with disdain. "It's not mine, and it's not jewelry."

"Er, okay. I'm still not sure how I can help you. Have you contacted the Sheriff's Department?" I point toward Sheriff Mack who I'm surprised to realize is watching me, but he quickly looks away. He must still be on pain medication from the accident because he's acting weird lately.

"This is not a matter for local law enforcement!" she snaps.

"Then you need to be clearer about what you're asking, because I still don't understand," I explain, trying to maintain my patience.

"The Precious Peridot is one of this town's most vital resources. Without it, I don't know how the town can go on!"

T hank you for reading **The Case of the Pilfering Poltergeist**!

Sign up for my email list here

https://mailchi.mp/9ebce0da866a/email-signup-list
Visit my website

biskinnerauthor.com
Follow me on Instagram **@bethiskinner** Facebook **@biskinnerauthor**